'You'll be here for Christmas, won't you?' It was more of a plea than a query.

She could see the way Jack drew in a deep breath. 'Do you want me to be?'

'Oh…yes.' Of course she wanted him to be here.

She wanted *him*. So much that it hurt.

'Then I will be here,' Jack said. His gaze held hers. 'Just for Christmas, Lizzie.' Bending his head, he kissed her softly.

Was he saying they could have this time together?

As a gift?

It wasn't enough. It could never be enough. But it was infinitely preferable to not having any of Jack at all.

It would have to be enough. Lizzie stood on tiptoe to return the kiss with one of her own.

'We'll just have to make the most of every moment of Christmas, then, won't we?'

THE NIGHT BEFORE BEFORE CHRISTMAS

BY
ALISON ROBERTS

Alison Roberts lives in Christchurch, New Zealand. She began her working career as a primary school teacher, but now juggles available working hours between writing and active duty as an ambulance officer. Throwing in a large dose of parenting, housework, gardening and pet-minding keeps life busy, and teenage daughter Becky is responsible for an increasing number of days spent on equestrian pursuits. Finding time for everything can be a challenge, but the rewards make the effort more than worthwhile.

CHAPTER ONE

'PLEASE, Mummy...*please*...'

The huge blue eyes were filled with such desperate longing, it was unbearable.

'But it'll be horribly crowded, darling. We'll have to stand in a big queue for heaven knows how long.'

'I don't mind.'

'We might be gone for hours.'

'Misty doesn't mind, either. Do you, Misty?'

Another set of blue eyes but without the sparkle. Framed by the same gorgeous, golden curls, but this face was much thinner and there were shadows caused by the kind of pain no child should have to endure. The brave smile as this little girl shook her head in agreement was even more unbearable. It was enough to create the unpleasant prickle of tears at the back of Lizzie's eyes.

She swallowed them away with a skill born of long practice.

'It's 'portant, Mummy. I have to tell Santa what me and Misty want for Christmas.'

'Christmas is weeks away, Holly. Santa will be there every day from now on. It's the first day of the big sale today and that's why it'll be so crowded. We could go next week.'

'*No-o-o.*'

'Why not?'

'Cos it's Santa's first day and he might 'member what I tell him and he might forget when he's listened to lots and lots of other girls and boys. Me and Misty's secret might fall out of his head, like things do for Nanna.'

There was a snort from the corner of the room, but no comment. Lizzie hid a smile. She also stifled a sigh, trying to think.

It would be overheated and stuffy in the famous department store, Bennett's. There would be a huge queue with dozens of children waiting with their parents for their turn to sit on Santa's knee and whisper secrets. Happy, excited, *healthy* children and she'd have to stand there for far too long. Feeling the pull back to this small hospital room. But if she stayed, she'd feel guilty. Holly needed her too and she was going to get even less of her mother's time in the next few weeks.

'For heaven's sake,' came a firm voice from the same direction the snort had come from. 'Go, Lizzie. You'll be seeing more than you want of four walls like this in a couple of days. I'll stay here with Misty.'

'Are you sure, Mum? You've done so much already today. You must be exhausted. How's your hip?'

The older woman smiled, looking up from a pile of felt fabric she was sorting in her lap. 'I'm fine. Think about yourself for once, love. Go and have some fun with Holly. Bring me back some of that lovely Bennett's shortbread and I'll be happy.'

Holly was whispering in her sister's ear and Misty

was nodding. Smiling as she whispered back. They both looked at their mother and the solemn expression on two small faces told Lizzie that the secret was of the utmost importance.

She had to swallow hard again. Her two precious daughters who should look identical but were becoming more different every day.

How ironic that she'd chosen Misty as the name for the twin who was fading away before their eyes.

What was the secret wish that Santa had to know about as soon as possible?

That this was going to work? That Misty would be well again?

Hope might be a vital ingredient in what made something successful. Lizzie took a deep breath. She smiled.

'Come on, then, Tuppence. Let's go and see Santa.'

Jack Rousseau had no idea whether he was heading in the right direction.

Why on earth had he thought he might as well pop into Bennett's because it was right beside the bank and get finding the only Christmas gifts he needed to purchase out of the way? He should have spent a pleasant Sunday morning in the markets last week, when he had still been in Paris, and found something original enough to make both his housekeepers smile.

Instead, he was here in London and it was freezing and grey outside and way too crowded and warm inside. And he only had an hour or so until he was due at the 'meet and greet' at Westbridge Park, the prestigious hospital where he was due to start his temporary specialist position tomorrow.

The sensible thing to do would be to give up and come back another time. Preferably when the sale had finished. Late at night, too, so there wouldn't be so many noisy children and pushchairs to avoid. He should have stayed downstairs and chosen something in the perfume department and ignored the flash of inspiration that had sent him in search of kitchenware. Now he was trapped on an escalator, looking down on a sea of humanity and Christmas decorations.

Christmas.

Was anybody quite as unlucky as he was in having the whole world building up expectations to a day that held a memory as unpleasant as the spectacular ending of a marriage? He had avoided the whole business now as far as humanly possible for many years. A bonus in the form of cash had always been suitable for the people he'd needed to find gifts for so why had he chosen this year to break his routine?

There had to be a thousand trees in this store. *Incroyable.* There was a whole forest of them when he stepped off at the top. Green trees. Silver and white ones. Even a fluorescent blue thing that looked very wrong. They were all covered with bows and balls and twinkling lights and it was all too much. Jack ducked between two of them and found himself in, of all places, the lingerie department.

Pausing to catch his breath and find an easy escape route, he found the shapely mannequins, wearing Christmas hats and very little else, quite a pleasant distraction. Jack was rather taken with a red and black striped bustier with built-in suspenders that were holding up some fishnet stockings.

A perfect Christmas gift for the woman with the right credentials. What a shame Danielle had given him that ultimatum only last week. She knew the rules, he explained silently to the mannequin, so why had she gone and ruined everything by demanding a commitment he would never make again? With a grimace that embraced both the current emptiness of his bed and the fact that he was trying to communicate telepathically with a plastic woman, Jack sighed and turned to scan the crowds once more, looking for a 'down' escalator.

There was a long queue of people making a human barrier halfway across this floor and Jack turned his head to find out what the attraction might be. A fashion parade perhaps? In the lingerie department?

No such luck. He should have guessed by the fact that everyone in this queue had small people attached to them. There was a Christmas grotto over there by the lifts and a Father Christmas was enthroned on a crimson velvet chair. A photographer was adjusting lights as a mother tried to persuade a toddler to sit still on Santa's knee to have his picture taken.

A nearby child was whining. 'When's *my* turn, Mum?'

Another was crying. The rising level of high-pitched, excited voices was starting to make him feel distinctly uncomfortable, like fingernails on a blackboard.

The stairs would be faster. Turning on all the charm he could muster, Jack edged rapidly through the press of humanity, excusing himself repeatedly. The vast majority of the people were women and they responded admirably to a bit of authority tempered with a smile.

That they continued to stare at him after he'd passed by went unnoticed.

He almost made it. If it hadn't been for the little grandma practically fainting in his arms, he would have been half way down the stairs by now.

Instead, he found himself searching for a chair. 'Is there somewhere she could sit down?' he asked the saleswoman who had come rushing to help.

'Here. This way.' The face over the trim black skirt and frilly white blouse was anxious. The woman, whose name tag said 'Denise', was holding aside the curtain that was being used to screen the back of the Christmas grotto.

The chair was solid and wooden and the elderly woman sank onto it with a relieved groan.

'Keep your head down for a moment,' Jack said. He supported her with one arm, using his free hand to find her wrist.

'Shall I call for an ambulance?' Denise asked.

'No!' The elderly woman shook her purple rinsed hair. 'Please don't do that.'

'Give us a minute,' Jack said. 'I'm a doctor.'

'Oh-h-h.' Denise smiled for the first time. 'That's lucky.'

Jack thought of the minutes ticking past and how hard it might be to find a taxi once he made it outside but he wasn't going to contradict Denise. He could feel a rapid and rather weak pulse in the wrist he was hold-ing and he noted the faint sheen of perspiration on the woman's pale face.

'What's your name?' he enquired.

'Mabel.'

'I'm Jack,' he told her. 'Dr Rousseau. Tell me, has anything like this ever happened to you before?'

'No. I'm as healthy as a horse. I don't want any fuss. I just…came over a bit funny, that's all.'

'Dizzy?'

'Oh…yes.'

'Sick?'

'Yes. I'm starting to feel a bit better now, though.'

'No pain in your chest?'

'No.'

'You're puffing a bit.'

'I walked up all those stairs. My great-grandson's here somewhere, with my daughter. He's waiting to see Father Christmas.'

This was where the man in the red suit must come when he was allowed a breather, Jack decided. There was a small table beside the chair with a carafe of water and some glasses.

'Do you think I could have a glass of that water, dear?' Mabel asked.

Denise did the honours. Jack stayed where he was, thinking through his options. If he could rule out anything serious, like a cardiac event, he could probably leave Mabel and escape downstairs. Or maybe they could take her downstairs. It was rather stuffy in this small, curtained space. He was in a corner and his back was right against one edge. Right beside the red velvet throne, judging by how clearly he could hear voices.

'Hello there, dear. What's *your* name?'

'Holly.'

'And how old are you, Holly?'

'I'm six.'

'And what it is you want for Christmas?'

'It's not just for me.' The six year old girl sounded so earnest she was breathless. 'It's for Misty, too.'

'Who's Misty?'

'My sister.'

'And how old is Misty?'

'She's six, too.'

'Oh…you must be twins.'

Santa didn't sound half as bright as Holly, Jack thought. He still had his fingers on Mabel's wrist and her pulse was jumping a bit. Maybe he should send for an ambulance. Just because she wasn't experiencing any chest pain, it didn't mean she wasn't having a heart attack. The pulse was faint enough to make him concerned about her blood pressure as well. Of course, if she'd nearly fainted, it would have dropped considerably but it didn't pick up in the next minute or so, he'd need to do something.

'How old are you, Mabel?'

'Eighty-three.'

'Are you on medication for anything?'

'Just my blood pressure. The doctor's given me some new pills for it. I just started them yesterday.'

'Hmm. That might well have something to do with how you're feeling. Can you remember the name of the pills?' he asked.

'They're in my purse. Oh, no…where *is* my purse?'

'You must have dropped it!' Denise exclaimed. 'Don't worry, I'll go and have a look right now.'

Jack watched with dismay as the saleswoman ducked through the curtain and disappeared. She might be gone for a long time and he could hardly abandon an elderly woman having a vagal episode, could he? He was trapped. Closing his eyes for a moment, he could hear that Holly was still chattering to Santa.

'It's cos we were born at Christmas. I'm Holly and she's Misty. Like, you know, misty-toe.'

Misty-toe? Jack felt his lips twitch and some of his frustration evaporated. He was stuck for the moment so he might as well try and enjoy it.

'And you and Misty want a daddy for Christmas, you said?'

A *daddy*? Jack blinked and started listening a lot more carefully.

'Yes, please. Is that OK? Mummy says we don't need one really but I'm sure she'd like it. You can manage that, can't you? I told Misty you could. She wanted to come too but she's too sick.'

'Ah… I'm sorry to hear that.'

So was Mabel. Her head was up and she was clearly eavesdropping on the secret conversation behind them as well. At the mention of the sick sister, she looked straight at Jack. Horrified? More like…expectant.

As if *he* could do anything about it. He was a specialist surgeon, not a paediatrician. Unless they needed new body parts transplanted, he didn't have anything to do with small people.

He had to admit he was getting curious about this child, though. It wasn't hard to straighten a little and move his head to where there was a gap in the curtain that would allow him to have a peek.

He could see the back of Santa's head and the arm that was around the child on his knee. He could see a mop of blonde curls around a very pretty face that was staring very intently at the man hearing her wish. She had the biggest, bluest eyes Jack had ever seen. Give her a set of wings and a little halo on a headband and this Holly would make a perfect Christmas angel.

How sad that she had a twin sister who was so sick.

Santa must be feeling the same way. He was certainly giving this child a little more time than others might have had.

'She's going to be all right. Mummy's hoping she'll get a really special Christmas present that will make her better, but you know what?'

'What?' The tone was wary.

Jack's interest was firmly piqued. A special Christmas present that would make her better? It was the sort of thing a parent for a child waiting on an organ to become available might say. Bit much to expect a miracle before Christmas if they were on the kind of waiting list the majority of his patients had to rely on, though.

'I think having a daddy would make her feel better. It would make us *all* feel better.'

'I'll…see what I can do.'

'He has to be nice,' Holly said firmly. 'And kind. And he has to be really, really nice to Mummy so she'll like him too. That's my mummy over there, see?'

Jack's head mirrored the turn that Santa's head made. The woman standing beside the photographer was un-mistakeably Holly's mother. An older version, really, with shoulder-length, blonde curly hair and a cute nose and, while it was far too far away to see the colour of her eyes, Jack just knew they would be as blue as a mid-summer sky. Mummy was curvy in all the right places, too. In fact, it was a bit of a puzzle why she was alone. Looking like that, surely she'd be fighting off potential daddies? What man wouldn't want to be really, really nice to her?

Apart from him, of course. He'd been there and done that and the failure was a huge black mark on a personal history that otherwise shone with achievement. A wise man did not repeat his mistakes.

Santa stared for a moment or two and Jack could hear him sigh as he turned back. Holly's head turned as well. Far enough to catch sight of Jack peering through the curtain.

'Ooh,' she squeaked. 'Who are *you*?'

Jack had to think fast. 'Just one of Santa's helpers,' he whispered.

'Are you a…nelf?'

'Yes.' Jack nodded. His smile seemed to come from a different place than usual. It felt…softer. 'That's it. I'm a nelf.'

'Why haven't you got a green hat?'

He was spared having to answer. The photographer was tapping his watch and the next woman in the queue was edging forward with a small boy who had a very expectant smile. It was clearly the next child's turn to tell Santa what he wanted for Christmas and Holly was distracted by the gentle nudge that was intended to dislodge her from her perch. Not that she was having any of it.

'He has to be nice to me and Misty as well as Mummy,' she told Santa hurriedly. 'That's 'portant. Uncle Nathan liked Mummy but he didn't like us, 'specially when Misty got sick, so Mummy told him to go away and never come back.'

'O-kay,' said Santa. 'I'll keep that in mind. But now it's time for—'

'Mummy said she wasn't sad because she loves *us* so much she doesn't need anybody else. She said we're the two best little girls in the *whole* world and I'm trying to be extra-good even when it's hard and everybody's crying because if you're good, you get want you want for Christmas, don't you?'

Why was everybody crying? Jack wondered. Was Misty's case hopeless?

He glanced at Mabel. *She* was crying.

'The poor wee pet,' she whispered.

'Mummy looks after everybody.' The voice was wobbling now. 'Me and Misty *and* Nanna. But there's nobody to take care of Mummy, is there? I'm still too little.'

The photographer was talking to Holly's mother, who nodded and marched forward.

'Come on, Holly. You've had your turn now.'

'But—'

'No "buts". Come on, we'll go and find that shortbread for Nanna.'

It was a grown-up version of the determination he'd been hearing in Holly's voice.

'Merry Christmas,' Santa intoned, but he didn't sound nearly as jolly as he probably should. 'Ho, ho, ho.'

Denise came back. She had a middle-aged woman with her who turned out to be Mabel's daughter.

The elderly woman was feeling much better. Her daughter said they were going to go straight to the doctor's on the way home. She thanked Jack profusely for his medical assistance. So did Denise as she dashed back to her duties.

Jack was free at last. He escaped from the back of the grotto. Heading for the stairs, he passed Denise, who'd been stopped by a customer's query.

The customer was none other than Holly's mother. Holly gave him a suspicious stare and must have communicated something through the hand she was holding because her mother turned her head to stare at him as well.

The eye contact was like nothing he'd ever experienced in his life. As though they *knew* each other. Intimately. A prickle of something he couldn't identify traced the length of his spine. His step faltered inexplicably. He covered the odd blip by glancing at his watch and seeing the time was more than enough incentive to keep moving. He had no choice, if he was going to have any chance of making his meeting on time.

Weirdly, what he was feeling now was a strong sense of disappointment. Because he would never know the end of the story about Holly and Misty and whether they would get what they wanted for Christmas.

No. It felt like more than that.

Almost as though he'd just lost something.

Something *'portant*.

'He's not really a nelf,' Holly muttered. 'He hasn't got a hat and he's too *big*.'

Lizzie was only half listening because Denise was trying to direct her to where she would find the shortbread she needed to take back to the hospital.

Who was too big?

That astonishingly good-looking man who'd just given her the oddest look? He had the most beautiful eyes she'd ever seen. Chocolate brown and…interested? No. It had been more than the kind of appreciative glance she was used to getting from men. It had been more like he was surprised to see her here. As if he knew her from somewhere else. That thought was just about as strange as whatever bee Holly had in her bonnet about elves.

If she'd met him before she would have most certainly not forgotten the encounter.

Keeping a firm hold on her daughter's hand, Lizzie went in search of shortbread. Holly was happy and so was she. In a little while their mission would be accomplished and she could get back to where she really needed to be.

Maybe later…much later, when she had a minute or two to herself, she would indulge in remembering those dark eyes. Relive that frisson of something amazing that she'd felt in that heartbeat when his eyes had touched hers.

A secret smile tweaked the corner of Lizzie's mouth. She'd have to save it for later but there was no reason not to indulge in a harmless little daydream. After all, who didn't need a touch of fantasy in their lives now and then?

CHAPTER TWO

THIS was payback.

On a cosmic scale. Punishment for the very real pleasure Lizzie had found last night, dreaming about a pair of chocolate-brown eyes.

She had never expected to see them again. Certainly not at close range. But here they were, on the other side of Dr Kingsley's desk.

'Who are you?'

Oh…Lord… It was supposed to come out as 'Who are *you*?' and not 'Who *are* you?', as if she remembered him and was desperate to know his name.

He wasn't smiling. In fact, he was giving her the same kind of odd look he had when he'd passed her in Bennett's department store yesterday.

'I'm Jack,' he told her. 'Jack Rousseau.'

His voice was as smooth as the rich chocolate his eyes made her think of. Just as dark, too. And there was a subtle hint of a very attractive accent. Rousseau? Was he French?

Lizzie's mouth went curiously dry and she dropped her gaze instantly. Not that it helped. He had both his hands on the desk, fiddling with the disc of a stethoscope lying on the blotter. Long, shapely fingers and hands, the backs of which were dusted with dark hair. Absolutely masculine hands but they looked very clever.

Sexy hands. Like the rest of this man whose name meant nothing to her. He was a complete stranger despite this odd feeling that she knew him. A two-second encounter in a crowded shop couldn't account for this feeling of familiarity but illicit fantasies in the privacy of her own bed certainly could.

This was appalling. She had to say something before her hesitation became any more obvious but Lizzie could feel a blush of gigantic proportions blooming. She felt somehow exposed. Vulnerable. Backed into a corner simply because she'd done a tiny thing for her own pleasure.

There was only one thing for it. She needed to come out fighting. Her chin rose sharply and she met those dark eyes directly.

'Where's Dr Kingsley?' she demanded.

As if to answer her sharp query, the door of the consulting room burst open.

'I'm so sorry, Lizzie,' Dave Kingsley said. 'I wanted to be here to introduce you to Jack myself.' He sent an apologetic smile to the younger man as he pulled another chair to that side of the desk. 'Didn't mean to abandon you for so long either.'

'Couldn't be helped,' Jack Rousseau said graciously. 'Emergencies happen.'

'Car accident to a patient of mine who had a transplant five years ago,' Dave explained to Lizzie, before turning back to his new colleague. 'Looks like he's

damaged the kidney, unfortunately, along with mess-
ing up his spleen and liver.'

'He'll be on his way to Theatre, then?'

'Yes. I might get a call. I said I wanted to have a look
before any call was made about removing the transplant.
Now…' The surgeon's smile signalled his change of
focus to Lizzie. 'You've obviously met Jack already.'

'Mmm…' Lizzie kept her gaze firmly on Dr
Kingsley.

'And he's explained why he's here?'

'We were about to get to that, I think,' Jack said.

Lizzie didn't have to look to know that he was smiling. She could hear it in his voice. He was finding this
amusing in some way? She could feel the skin on her
forehead tightening as she frowned.

'Let me do the honours, then,' Dave said. 'Mr
Rousseau…Jack…is very well known for his expertise in abdominal transplant surgery, Lizzie. Westbridge
Park has been trying to lure him away from his Paris
base for some time but the best we've been able to manage is to persuade him to spend a month or so giving a
series of lectures and working with other surgeons in
some individualised training programmes. I'm one of
them, I'm delighted to say.'

It would have been impolite not to shift her gaze to
acknowledge the apparently famous expert. To nod, at
least, as a sign of respect. Wiping the frown from her
face was a bit more of an ask. Having their paths cross
again like this still seemed a rather unfortunate twist
of fate given her enthusiastic foray into the world of
fantasy last night.

Her frown was noted.

'I'm not really as young as I look,' Jack Rousseau said kindly. 'I'm thirty-six and I can assure you that I've had considerable experience in cases such as yours.'

Was he planning to take over her surgery? *Misty's* surgery?

'I'm more than happy with Dr Kingsley's experience, thank you,' she announced. 'For myself *and* for my daughter.'

'Heavens above, Lizzie,' Dave put in. 'I'm not about to hand you over. Though I have invited Jack to supervise and possibly assist in the surgery if that's acceptable to you. Never hurts to have an extra set of eyes and hands, particularly if they happen to be regarded as the best in the world.'

The sound from the other man in the room was a protest of modesty. 'The real reason I want to be there,' Jack told her, 'is that I'd like your permission to film the surgeries for use in my upcoming lectures.'

Lizzie stared at him. So he was thirty-six? Yes, she could see the fine lines that life had etched around his eyes and the first hint of the odd silver hair in those dark waves. He had the aura that only came with a combination of intelligence and power and she could imagine how skilled those hands must be. Oddly, the memory of those hands made a sudden heat bloom in her belly. It was disconcertingly difficult to drag her gaze away.

'I can assure you that it won't compromise your care in any way,' Jack continued. 'I have a highly skilled cameraman who's worked with me in many major hospitals across Europe and in the States.'

Lizzie blinked at that. He must be famous and to be

that famous at such a relatively young age must mean that he was seriously good at what he did.

And this was on top of being by far the most attractive man she'd ever been this close to. Certainly the first chance encounter she'd ever indulged in fantasising about.

That initial embarrassment had faded but did she really want him to be involved in any way with her medical procedures? Being in Theatre while she was lying there with her abdomen exposed?

The very idea made her squirm uncomfortably.

Jack could see that Lizzie wasn't exactly thrilled by the idea.

He sat back, toying with the stethoscope hanging around his neck, listening to Dave Kingsley explain how her case had been chosen out of all the ones they'd reviewed yesterday afternoon for just this purpose.

He could understand why she was uncomfortable with having to deal with an unexpected new development. This morning's appointment was a crucial point in the journey she was on and lives were at stake on this journey. Specifically, the life of a six-year-old girl. What he could see in front of him was a mother who was prepared to do whatever it would take to keep her family safe.

She didn't need a father for her children because she loved them so much she didn't need anybody else. Because they were the best little girls in the whole world.

He'd been right, of course. Her eyes were as blue as her daughter's.

'I don't care about myself,' she was saying, 'but I'm not having Misty turned into some kind of reality TV show.'

'It's nothing like that,' Dave assured her. 'She won't be identified and it's purely for the purpose of training other surgeons.'

Lizzie shot a suspicious glance in his own direction and Jack tried to look suitably serious. She was a fighter, this one. Determination like that, especially on behalf of someone else, was admirable. It was hard not to give her an encouraging smile.

She was also...*absolument magnifique*.

Quite possibly, the most attractive woman Jack had ever seen. So soft and feminine with those curves and the shining waves of her hair. It was her eyes that really caught him, though. They were utterly compelling. The urge to win her trust and thereby win permission to be part of the team that could remove some of the sadness from those eyes was so powerful it made him tighten his grip on the stethoscope he was fiddling with. The plastic cover on the disc popped off and provided him with a momentary and probably very timely distraction.

He shouldn't be so aware of Lizzie like this. It was unprecedented. Unprofessional. Jack took a steadying breath as he clicked the clear plastic circle back into place. It was only then that he noticed Dave getting out of his chair. He was reading his pager.

'Have a chat to Jack about it before you make a decision,' he was saying to Lizzie. 'We certainly won't do anything you're not happy with. Excuse me for a few minutes. They want a decision made about this kidney. It shouldn't take long.'

And then he was gone and Jack was again alone with Lizzie. He smiled at her.

'Do you have any questions you'd like to ask, Mrs Matthews?'

'Yes, I do, Dr Rousseau.'

Jack raised his eyebrows to encourage her.

'Dr Kingsley said you chose this case as being perfect for filming.'

'This is true.'

'He said you spent all afternoon reviewing every case available.'

'Also true.'

Her gaze was accusing. 'So how come I saw you in town, then? In Bennett's?'

She remembered him. Jack tried to ignore the pulse of something pleasant that was warming his gut. 'I was trying to fit in a bit of Christmas shopping.' Any further personal-type conversation was entirely unnecessary but Jack found himself continuing nonetheless. 'Unsuccessful, unfortunately. Partly due to those crowds but mainly thanks to my interlude of impersonating a nelf.'

Lizzie gave her head a small shake that send a wayward curl onto her cheek. She pushed it back. 'An *elf*? Holly said something about elves when she saw you but I had no idea what she was talking about.'

She was staring at Jack, clearly puzzled. There was a question in her eyes, too. One that carried an expectation. He had something she wanted.

An explanation? He could give her that, no problem. He could give her a lot more than that, if she would let him. He could potentially make a real contribution to giving her what she wanted more than anything—her child's health.

For some reason, this case was special. So special there was a distinct niggle at the back of his mind that it was unprofessional to want to be involved *this* much. Was it because the consultant surgeon he was working with felt the same way? Maybe the concern expressed when they had been discussing it yesterday had been contagious. Whatever the cause was, it had certainly never happened to Jack before and the pull was too powerful to resist. Maybe the 'nelf' was his ace card.

'An elderly woman became unwell after climbing the stairs. I needed somewhere to look after her and one of the saleswomen showed us a private space that happened to be Santa's rest area. Curtained off behind where he was sitting. Holly saw me through the gap in the curtain and wanted to know who I was and I said I was a helper.'

'Oh-h…' Lizzie was smiling now. Just a small smile but it was encouraging. 'I suppose it was her that decided you were an elf.'

'I got demerit points because I didn't have a hat.'

The smile widened. Then it faded and Lizzie's eyes widened. 'You were right there?'

'Yes.'

'So you heard what Holly was saying to Santa?'

'Ah…' The truth was probably obvious in his face. Or the way he diverted his gaze hurriedly. He couldn't tell her what he'd overheard, could he? Apart from the potential for mutual embarrassment, he was just getting further and further away from what needed to be discussed, which was Lizzie and Misty's surgeries and the permission for him to be involved.

In an effort to cover his discomfort, he pulled an impressive set of patient notes from the side of his desk to sit right in front of him. He even opened it to the latest sheaf of notes and test results, knowing that consent forms for both the surgery and the filming rights had been tucked behind them. When he glanced up, however, he could see that Lizzie was having none of the change of direction. It reminded him very strongly of the way Holly had refused to budge from Santa's knee.

'You're smiling,' Lizzie said accusingly. 'You *do* know.'

Jack sighed. He was probably blowing his chance of persuading Lizzie to trust him here and welcome his involvement in her case but Holly deserved respect for her determination and courage. So did Lizzie. He wasn't about to betray a small girl but Lizzie deserved nothing less than the truth.

'Yes, I do know,' he acknowledged reluctantly.

She leaned forward a fraction, clearly expecting to hear more. Her lips parted slightly in anticipation and she even moistened the lower one with the tip of a very pink tongue.

Jack felt a groan somewhere deep inside his body. One that could not be allowed to form properly, never mind escape.

'But I can't reveal anything,' he added firmly.

Lizzie's eyebrows shot up. 'Why not?'

'Nelf law, I'm afraid. We're expressly forbidden to reveal Christmas wishes. If we do, they lose any power they have to come true.'

Lizzie's lips twitched. She was silent for a moment and then it was her turn to sigh. 'Are you at least allowed to give an opinion on whether or not this wish might be granted?'

Jack rubbed his chin thoughtfully. 'I think that's permissible. And, yes, I think the odds on that wish being granted are quite high. Possibly not before Christmas, though.'

Lizzie's face fell.

'But it *will* happen,' he added hurriedly. 'I'm sure of it.'

How could it not happen when this woman was, quite simply, adorable?

If *he* could see that, as a man who had no interest whatsoever in finding a wife, surely she would be able to pick and choose from any available male that happened to come into her orbit? Not that it was any of his business, of course, and it was far too personal a topic to allow himself to even think about it for a moment longer.

He cleared his throat and tore his gaze away, looking down at the notes. 'Dave should be back soon. It's going to be a busy day for you with your final run of tests like the final cross-match and ECG and so on. I don't want to hold things up, so if you're really not happy about having me in Theatre, I'll leave you to it.'

He risked another glance to see her looking torn. Small, white teeth were worrying that full bottom lip and huge, blue eyes were fixed on him with a very searching gaze. 'So it's abdominal transplants you specialise in, Dr Rousseau?'

'Please, call me Jack. I dislike too much formality. May I call you Lizzie?'

She nodded. The pink flush on her cheeks was appealing.

He made his tone friendly but nodded in what he hoped was a serious, professional manner. 'Indeed I do specialise in abdominal transplants. Kidneys, livers, the occasional whole bowel, in fact.' He spoilt the serious effect a little by smiling at her. 'I think kidneys are my favourite. The results of a successful transplant are so rewarding, particularly when it's from a living donor. A case like yours in not uncommon because there are many parents who are willing to donate an organ or part of one for their child but it's not something I've documented for lecture purposes yet.'

'And you want to document my case?'

'I think so. I'd like to run through it quickly with you now, if you are agreeable. Just while we're waiting for Dr Kingsley to return?'

He was a stranger, this man, and yet Lizzie's faith in him was growing by the minute.

Trust had been won.

Because of 'nelf law'? How absurd was that? Except it had nothing to do with his sense of humour or ability to get out of a tight corner. It was to do with the kind of man who would stop and help an elderly woman who wasn't well. Even more convincingly, one who was prepared to keep the secret of a six-year-old child. Holly might not realise it but her secret was obviously safe.

It was also because of his obvious integrity. They only employed the best here and if Dave Kingsley trusted him on a professional level then she wasn't about to question his judgement. There was a more tangible level to his professionalism, however. One that made her feel like he genuinely cared about his patients.

Here he was, reviewing her file and reading personal information that she wouldn't have dreamed of sharing with a stranger on first acquaintance, but it didn't feel intrusive.

'So…normal pregnancy and delivery when you were…twenty-four?'

'That's right.'

'And the twins' development seemed normal for the first two to three years.'

'Yes.'

He read on in silence for a moment and then he looked up. 'Two toddlers, one of whom was sick, and you're a single mother? That must have been a tough time.'

She could see sympathy in his eyes. And a gentleness that made her want to cry. She pressed her lips together and looked away with a simple nod of response. She had learned to cope alone. She didn't need this man's sympathy.

The silence lingered a moment longer and then she heard Jack clear his throat again.

'The diagnosis of hypoplastic and dysplastic kidneys was made when Misty was three…but she didn't go into end-stage renal failure until earlier this year. And she's been on dialysis for the last three months?'

'Yes.'

'But not peritoneal.'

'No. I…didn't want her to have the catheter inserted

in her tummy and do home dialysis and have to worry about infection and things. I'd already passed the first compatibility tests and there was no question about not doing a transplant. We hoped that it could be done before the need for dialysis but...what with shifting in with my mother to be closer to the hospital and Misty getting sick and then I caught that bug and...'

Her litany of woes ended as the door opened and her surgeon came back into the room. He looked at both of them and then at the opened case notes.

'Another review?'

Jack nodded. 'Just in case Lizzie is agreeable to the filming.'

She could still see the sympathy in his face. The gentleness. And something else. He looked as though he really wanted to be a part of this. As though he genuinely cared.

'I'm agreeable,' she said quietly.

'Excellent.' Dave Kingsley sounded delighted. He leaned across his desk to pull pads of requisition forms from a plastic tray. 'You'll need a chest X-ray and an ECG to sign off your fitness for surgery. We'll also do an ultrasound of your kidney and bladder and run off the final blood tests for kidney function and cross-match.'

'But we've done that so many times already. I'm as close a match as could be hoped for from a parent.' Lizzie found herself smiling at Jack. 'Holly wanted to give Misty one of her kidneys. She was really cross when we told her you had to be eighteen years old.'

He smiled back at her. 'They're identical twins, yes?'

'Yes. They…don't look exactly the same any more, though. Holly's taller and…' And so much healthier.

'She might well catch up after the transplant,' Dr Kingsley said. 'And it's good to know there might be a perfect match down the track if things don't go perfectly this time. You do understand there's no guarantee of success, don't you?'

Lizzie nodded. 'I know the statistics are better for live donations and the treatment for any episodes of rejection are getting better all the time. The odds are in our favour.'

'Very true,' Jack put in. 'But that's why we do a last-minute cross-match to check compatibility again. Just in case any antibodies have sneaked in as a result of the illnesses you've both had recently.'

Lizzie nodded again. She crossed the fingers of one hand in her lap, covering them with her other hand so that neither of these highly trained surgeons would see such a childish action.

'I'd prefer to run the standard checks again for Hep B and C and HIV as well, even though I see that your last results were fine.' Jack was smiling at her again. 'I like to tick all these boxes myself for cases I'm involved with.' He glanced at his colleague. 'If you don't see it as interference?'

'Heavens, no. Sounds like a good quality control measure to me. Feel free to keep ticking boxes in Theatre as well,' Dave said.

Lizzie could swear that Jack gave her the ghost of a wink. 'There are so many boxes to tick in there, they need a supply of extra pens. Sterilised, of course.'

Dave was pulling sheets of loose paper from the case

notes. 'I have the consent forms here if you're ready to sign them?'

Lizzie nodded.

Jack frowned slightly. 'You've discussed this already?'

'I know about the possible complications,' Lizzie said.

'Lizzie's a nurse,' Dave explained. 'She worked in Theatre for quite a while before moving to a job in the emergency department.'

'I'm not going to change my mind,' she added firmly.

Jack raised a single eyebrow that told them both this was one of his boxes and her breath huffed out in a resigned sigh.

'OK. Go ahead. I've only worked part time in a general practice since the twins were born so I guess I'm pretty rusty.'

There was an appreciative gleam in Jack's eyes now that suggested, rather flatteringly, that he thought it would take more than some time away from the front line for her mental wheels to collect rust. Clearly it wasn't enough to persuade him to make an exception, however. And that was good. A careful surgeon was a good surgeon. Even if he was only there in a supervisory capacity she wouldn't be impressed by someone who wanted to cut corners.

'The first thing I'll say is that death from a kidney donation is exceptionally rare—approximately 0.03 per cent—but it has happened so I have to mention it.'

Lizzie nodded. It was a risk she was more than prepared to take. The alternative of staying alive and watching her precious child die was unthinkable.

'Other complications might include you needing a blood transfusion during surgery, a small degree of lung collapse, blood clots in your legs or lungs, pneumonia and a UTI or wound infection.'

Lizzie was reaching for the consent form.

Dave pointed to a line on the document. 'This states that I'll do the procedure laparoscopically, which should give you a much faster recovery rate, but if it's difficult for any reason, it gives me permission to go for an open procedure. That would give you a bigger scar and mean that you were in hospital for about a week instead of three to four days.'

'And Misty? How long will she need to be in hospital for?'

'Probably at least two weeks. She'll still need dialysis until the new kidney settles in and we'll want to make sure everything's fine before she goes home.'

'But it's possible she could be home for Christmas?' Lizzie asked anxiously.

'Absolutely.'

Oh…yes… Dr Jack Rousseau's smile was gorgeous, all right. It wrapped itself around Lizzie like a hug as she signed the necessary permissions for both her own surgery and Misty's.

Dave Kingsley's voice sounded oddly distant for a few seconds.

'Sorry, what was that?' she said.

'I said we'll send you out to see the nurse. She'll give you a gown and pop you in an examination room. We'll give you a bit of a once-over and then send you off for the rest of your tests.'

The warm glow that the visiting surgeon's smile had

given her faded so fast Lizzie was left with a faint chill that trickled down her spine. A physical examination? With this Dr Rousseau watching or…worse….doing it himself? She wasn't bothered by the thought of him seeing parts of her she'd never see herself when she was being operated on. She'd be asleep after all. But to be awake and so aware of him? To have him maybe pressing his hand on her bare stomach?

Oh, Lord! Why did he have to be so young?

So impossibly good looking? And…*nice*, damn it.

And why, oh, why had she let herself step into fantasyland in the dead of night and imagine just what it would be like to be touched by him?

Maybe her reaction was obvious in the way Lizzie was prising herself off her chair to follow Dr Kingsley's instructions.

'I'll leave you to it,' she heard Jack say. 'I'll catch up with the test results later today before we go and visit Misty.'

'Misty Matthews? She's in Room 3. You must be Dr Rousseau.' The nurse's tone was awed. 'Welcome to Westbridge.'

'Thank you. I'm due to meet Dave Kingsley to review this patient. Is he here already?'

'He was but he got a call up to the ICU. He said to look after you until he got back. Would you like a coffee?'

Jack shook his head. 'My time is a little limited. I'll go and see Misty now, if I may.'

'Of course. This way.'

The whole family was in the small room.

'This is Dr Rousseau,' Lizzie told the child in the bed. 'He's the doctor who's going to help Dr Kingsley take Mummy's kidney out and give it to you.'

'Hi, there.' Jack took a step closer to the bed. His shirt collar felt inexplicably tight and he found himself loosening his tie.

He never felt comfortable around small people. They could see too much and had no hesitation in saying whatever came into their heads and sometimes he had no idea how to respond. Or he didn't understand what on earth they were talking about. Or, worse, they'd cry. A lot.

Misty wasn't crying. She wasn't saying anything either. Lizzie was sitting in a chair beside the bed and Holly was right beside the pillow, tilted in as if she wanted to be as close as possible to her twin. The resemblance between the twins was striking. Or maybe it was the difference between them that was making Jack feel like there wasn't quite enough oxygen in this private room.

Or it could be due to the way Lizzie was sitting, with her arms on Misty's bed as she leaned forward to talk to the little girl. The way it was making her cleavage so obvious, pushing mounds of skin that looked incredibly smooth and soft into a line of sight he couldn't avoid to save himself.

Well, he could, but that would mean meeting the intense stares that were coming from both Holly and the older woman in the armchair by the window.

'You're going to help with *both* operations?' The older woman sounded as wary as she looked.

'Not at the same time.' Jack tried his most charming smile. 'Lizzie's first and then we go next door to Misty.'

The sniff wasn't impressed. 'Doesn't Misty need a paediatric specialist for her surgery?'

'Mum…' Lizzie sounded embarrassed. 'We talked about this. And you heard what the nurses said about… Jack.' Her quick glance in his direction was appealingly shy. 'It wasn't that I was checking up on you or anything. They were all talking about how famous you are in your field and how lucky we are to have you involved in our case.'

Lizzie's mother was giving her a stern look. 'Oh… *Jack*, now, is it?'

'We got to know each other this morning,' Jack said. 'Didn't we, Lizzie?'

Her head bobbed. A touch of pink bloomed on her cheeks and she could only meet his gaze for a heartbeat. Jack turned his head back to her mother and extended his hand.

'Jack Rousseau,' he said, with another smile. 'I'm delighted to meet you, Mrs…'

'Donaldson.' Her gaze took a moment to meet his. She had been watching Lizzie rather carefully and she clearly hadn't missed any undercurrent. It was definitely too hot in this room. 'Maggie,' she continued. 'Excuse me if I don't get up.'

'Mum's got a bad hip,' Lizzie said.

'I'm sorry to hear that.' Jack leaned down to make it easy to shake hands. Maggie's grip was surprisingly firm.

'I'm on the waiting list for a replacement.' The tone was matter-of-fact. Her own physical impairment was an inconvenience that was being dealt with. 'Next year some time. Perhaps.'

The implications were not lost on Jack. This was Lizzie's mother. The grandmother of the two father-less girls. Lizzie had moved in with her mother to keep Misty closer to this hospital and must be relying on her heavily for help. Being in hospital herself for at least the next few days would make Maggie's role even more vital. There were pressures going on here that were huge. Important. Maybe he could have a word with someone in Orthopaedics and see if there was any way of getting a priority sticker put on Maggie's case.

A warning bell sounded somewhere in his head. Just how involved was he trying to get here? Maggie's hip was well outside the orbit of what he should be concen-trating on. He was here because of Misty. And Lizzie and their complementary surgeries that he was going to document. Whatever else was going on in his patients' worlds had absolutely nothing to do with *him*.

'It's Dr Kingsley that is actually doing the surger-ies,' he told Maggie. 'Lizzie has kindly agreed to let me document them on film so that I can use them for the purpose of giving lectures. The reason for the same surgeon doing both of the operations is to have things matched up perfectly. Think of it like a jigsaw puzzle. If I cut a piece out myself, I can put it back in exactly the right place. That is something I want to be able to demonstrate to other surgeons.'

'He likes to tick all the boxes.' Lizzie nodded. 'For himself.'

'I'm not a jigsaw puzzle,' Misty said. 'I'm…me.'

Jack moved back to the bed. He loosened his tie a little more. He even undid the top button of his shirt. 'You are, indeed,' he told Misty. 'And I'm Dr Jack. How are you feeling?'

Misty said nothing. Was it too general a question for a child? The look he was receiving made him feel as though it had been a stupid question. And maybe it was. Misty's arm was heavily bandaged and plastic tubes snaked from under the covers to the dialysis machine that was whirring quietly as it did its job to make sure her blood was as clean as possible before tomorrow's surgery. She was pale and thin and was probably quite used to feeling a lot less than well.

He tried again. 'Does anything hurt?'

'No.'

'Are you worried about the operation?'

'No. The nurse showed me all about it with the teddy bear. And Mummy says you and Dr Dave are going to take the best care of me.'

'Did she?' Jack couldn't help shifting his gaze to Lizzie. He met a very steady look. One that said she was trusting him but he'd better not let her down.

Fair enough. He didn't intend to.

'I'm going to read your chart,' he told Misty. 'And see what they tell me about all the tests you had today. Dr...Dave will be here soon so that we can talk about you and Mummy and make sure we're all set for tomorrow morning.'

'Are you going to read Mummy's chart too?' It was Holly who asked the question.

Jack smiled at her. 'I've already done that.'

'Did I pass?' Lizzie's tone was carefully casual.

'With flying colours.' The atmosphere in the room lightened just a little. 'And when I've read Misty's I'm going to give her a quick check-up. Unless Dr Dave is back here by then.'

It took a few minutes to get himself up to speed with the chart and the latest results in Misty's notes. He was aware of Lizzie moving around the room, straightening things up, and of the twins having a whispered conversation that nobody else could hear.

When he finished, he nodded in satisfaction and unhooked the stethoscope from around his neck. 'Can I have a listen to your heart and lungs?' he asked Misty.

He had to push aside the memory of how he had avoided doing that for Lizzie this morning. Because he knew it would be unprofessional to be so aware of the warmth that would come from that amazing skin if he got too close? He'd been right to keep his distance. When she'd moved away from the bed, she'd been forced to brush past him rather closely due to the size of the room and he couldn't help noticing a compelling scent that had nothing to do with any perfume she was wearing. He was still trying to bury the memory of it.

Good grief. The look he found being bestowed on him by both the twins was identical. If he didn't know better, he could swear they knew exactly what he'd been trying so hard not to think about. And children *could* sense things, couldn't they? Like animals could sense fear.

In perfect unison, the twins stopped staring at him and looked at each other. For a moment there was a silent communication going on and Jack could feel the intensity. Then they both nodded and looked back at him.

And smiled.

CHAPTER THREE

THERE was no real reason for Jack to go and visit Lizzie the next afternoon.

Her surgery had been completed this morning and he had been nothing more than an observer. Dave Kingsley's work on both Lizzie and Misty had been of excellent quality and had needed no intervention of any kind on his part.

The filming had gone without hitch for both surgeries as well and now all Jack needed to do was edit the footage and write up the notes he would need to accompany the lectures due to start next week. He needed follow-up details for how the patients progressed after surgery, of course, but he could easily get that from talking to Dave. Or reviewing the medical notes.

He wanted to thank Lizzie again for giving her permission to film but it was hardly appropriate to do it when she was in her immediate post-surgical recuperation. He should wait until a later date. In a few days, perhaps, when she would be on the point of being discharged. Or even later, when he would probably find her visiting Misty and helping to care for the small girl until she, too, was well enough to go home.

So why had he abandoned the video equipment and half-written notes in the temporary office he'd been assigned in Dave Kingsley's department? Why hadn't he paged Kingsley and asked how his patients were doing or made arrangements to accompany the other surgeon when he did his evening rounds?

He told himself he didn't want to interrupt anything important. That he might well come across Dave or one of his registrars if he wandered in the direction of the ward. He even convinced himself that, seeing as he was in the vicinity, he might as well pop his head around the door and say hello to Lizzie.

She was in a small, private room near the nurses' station. And she was awake. She saw him the moment he came into view and the look on her face suggested that seeing a surgeon associated with Misty's case might be due to bad news arriving. It had been several hours since her surgery but not so long since Misty had been taken to Recovery and then the paediatric intensive care unit. Had Lizzie been awake long enough to be told the good news? Or, if she had, had her head been clear enough to remember the details?

He couldn't very well just stand in the doorway. He had to move closer and find something to say that would take away the flash of fear darkening her eyes and making her lips tremble.

Jack tried to smile but, weirdly, his lips refused to cooperate. 'Mission accomplished,' he said quietly.

Lizzie burst into tears.

Oh…God. What was he supposed to do now?

He didn't do tears. He could understand them, of course, and even sympathise with the grief or sadness they represented. Unthinkable to indulge in such an outward sign of weakness himself, however, and if he was honest, it was probably the key thing that put him off babies and children so resoundingly. Crying was such a messy process. And noisy. And...and...*needy*. And crying women always wanted something from him that he couldn't give them.

Jack looked hopefully over his shoulder but no nurse materialised to help him out. Where was Lizzie's mother? Stepping closer to reach for the call bell, he spotted the box of tissues on the bedside cabinet. OK, maybe he couldn't give Lizzie what she might need emotionally but there was no excuse not to do something practical that might help. He snatched a couple from the box and pressed them into Lizzie's closest hand. Carefully, because she still had an IV port taped to the back of it.

'It's *good* news,' he reassured her. 'Couldn't be better.'

Lizzie nodded. And sobbed as though her heart was breaking. She blew her nose on the tissues but the tears continued to flow.

Jack pulled out more tissues. A huge handful. Lizzie pressed them to her face and made some hiccupping sounds. A muffled word emerged between the hiccups.

'S-s-sorry.'

'Don't be daft.' Shifting from one foot to the other, Jack was feeling increasingly uncomfortable. Needing to move but knowing he couldn't possibly leave her alone like this, he perched himself on one hip on the edge of her bed. He would wait it out.

Lizzie's leg was under the covers, a solid bar that

would be pressed against his hip if he leaned back even slightly. The almost contact seemed to flick a switch inside him and suddenly it was easy to know what to do. He reached over her legs for the hand that wasn't clutching tissues. Small, delicate fingers curled around his and held on, warm and strong.

Any moment now Lizzie's mother would probably come in. Maybe Dave would arrive to check on his patient. Or a nurse would bustle in to check on her patient's vital signs and he'd be able to hand over this somewhat unorthodox semi-professional interaction.

Until then, however, he might as well give it his best shot. Without thinking, he stroked the back of Lizzie's hand with his thumb to get her attention.

'Misty came through like a little trouper,' he told her. 'She's in the paediatric intensive care unit now and still asleep but she's looking comfortable. And everything's looking just as I would hope. Dave did a brilliant job. Textbook stuff, perfect for filming and, believe me, I had a lot of boxes that needed ticking.'

There was a new sound from Lizzie. Still distinctly damp but definitely happier. A kind of gurgle that sounded like laughter. Her face appeared from behind the tissues, sporting a wobbly smile.

'I'm *so* happy,' she informed Jack.

His own smile came back from wherever he'd lost it. 'I can tell.'

He might be making light of her reaction but there was no doubting the very real joy in that smile. It lit up her face. No, actually, it lit up the entire room and the joy was astonishingly contagious. Jack couldn't remember when he'd last felt this happy himself. It was far more than the satisfaction of a job well done. This went deeper, tapping into long-lost memories or something.

You'd never get sick of seeing a smile like that, he thought. You'd be stupid not to do everything in your power to make sure you saw it as often as possible.

It began to dawn on him just how long they'd been doing nothing but smiling at each other. It was also only then that Jack realised he was still holding Lizzie's hand. He gave it a tiny squeeze, let it go and cleared his throat.

'How are *you* feeling?'

'I'm fine. Is Misty really doing well?'

'Absolutely. I would never be less than honest with you, Lizzie.'

Her gaze searched his and, finally, she gave a slow nod. She believed him.

'Thank God,' she whispered, her eyes drifting shut. Then they snapped open. 'And you, of course. Oh, help...have I even said thank you properly? I can't remember...'

Her smile had been thanks enough for anybody. Undeserved, in his case. 'You've got nothing to thank me for,' he assured her. 'And Dave will be back to see you before long, I'm sure. I might go and find out where he is for myself. Can I really tell him you're feeling all right?'

'I'm fine,' Lizzie repeated, but then she sighed and a furrow appeared on her forehead. 'A bit sore. Kind of tired.'

'Having a kidney removed is major surgery even when it's done via laparoscope. I'd be very surprised if you weren't feeling pretty wobbly right now.' On this occasion, he was quite prepared to forgive and forget the crying jag.

Judging by the way she caught her bottom lip between her teeth, he would have been better not to have said anything. Shame he wasn't still holding her hand so that he could give it another reassuring squeeze.

'I do apologise for the waterworks. You're not going to believe this but I hardly ever cry. I have no idea where that all came from.'

'From being bottled up for a very long time, I expect.' Again, Jack experienced a strong regret that he'd let go of her hand already. 'I do believe you, Lizzie. I think you're very strong and you've had more than any mother should have had to deal with. Years of it now. No wonder it's come flooding out with a bit of good news. Especially in the aftermath of a general anaesthetic.'

'Flooding's the word for it,' Lizzie muttered. She closed her eyes again, sinking a little further back on her pillows. 'Maybe you're right. I have tried to be strong. For the girls. And Mum. She's been a total rock for me ever since Jon died.'

This was none of his business. It had nothing to do with any kind of patient care. It didn't even have anything to do with the kind of background detail Jack liked to sprinkle his lectures with to make things more personal and interesting but he ignored the warning bell and asked anyway.

'How old were the twins when they lost their dad?'

'He didn't even get to celebrate their first birthday.' A huge tear came from beneath a closed eyelid and trickled down the side of Lizzie's nose. 'They won't have any memories of him except for photographs. And news clippings.'

'News clippings?'

'He was a hero.' Lizzie gave a huge sniff. 'A fireman who died in the line of duty. He went back into a house because some kids said their father was inside. The roof collapsed on top of him. Turned out the father was down the road in the pub and it had been his cigarette that fell down the back of the couch and started the fire.' Her eyes opened and Jack was struck by the incredible depth of colour. And the sadness. 'He *was* a hero but you know what? I'd rather my girls had a dad.'

Jack could hear the echo of a small girl's voice in the back of his mind. Telling Santa that she and her sister wanted a daddy for Christmas. That she thought it would make Mummy feel better too.

The shoes of a man who'd gone into a burning building to save a stranger would be hard to fill. Jack could almost feel sorry for any man who tried. But if he succeeded, he would win Lizzie. He couldn't feel sorry for him now. He could almost feel…envious?

Good grief. He looked at his watch. Surely there was somewhere else he needed to be by now? He had those lecture notes to write up. Phone calls to make to arrange to meet the other surgeons he was expecting to mentor over the next couple of months. Probably more than a hundred emails that would need attention.

'How's the pain level? I can check whether Dave has charted additional pain relief for you, if you like.'

'No…I don't want to be too fuzzy when I go and see Misty.'

'That won't be till tomorrow morning at the earliest. I'm sure that complete bed rest has been ordered overnight. That's certainly what my patients would be getting.'

'But—'

'Misty's asleep, Lizzie. Being extremely well cared for. She'll be on sedation overnight. You can be there when she wakes up.'

'But—'

A nurse bustled into the room. 'Oh…Mr Rousseau! I didn't know *you* were here. We're short-staffed and flat out at the moment.'

Her tone suggested she would have been in the room a lot sooner if she had known he was there. Was it unprofessional to be glad she hadn't known?

Quite likely, but it paled in comparison to sitting on a patient's bed, holding her hand and grinning at her like an idiot for goodness knew how long. Or even worse, feeling envious of some non-existent man who might become Lizzie's partner and a father figure to her daughters at some point in the future. The sooner he got things back on track the better. His career was his life and always would be. There was no room for anyone or anything else. His choice. End of story.

'I actually came by to try and catch up with Dr Kingsley. Is he around?'

'Just down the corridor, in Room 1. As far as I know, Lizzie's next on the list for a check-up. Shall I tell him you're here?'

Whatever drugs were in her system from the pain control or as an aftermath from the anaesthetic were doing strange things to Lizzie. Or maybe it was the sheer exhaustion that followed in the wake of her emotional release that was responsible for this peculiar, out-of-body experience.

The flash of anger at having her request to see Misty denied was long gone. She was too tired to feel angry and, in any case, she wasn't about to let anyone stop her from seeing her daughter. They could wheel her down in her bed if necessary, for heaven's sake. None of the medical staff around here seemed to understand how important it was. Dr Kingsley had been just as horrified as Jack had been at the idea of her being moved anywhere just yet.

She couldn't really be angry with either of them, could she? Dave Kingsley had apparently done a brilliant job with the surgeries. And Jack…well, he'd been nice enough to sit there and hold her hand while she'd bawled her eyes out.

There was a cringe factor there, with him having seen her looking her absolute worst. She might have to come up with a new fantasy to exorcise it. One in which Jack would see her in a pretty, floaty dress with her make-up and hair looking perfect. Where there was soft music playing in the background and he was taking her hand to lead her onto the dance floor.

The feel of his hand wouldn't be fantasy. She knew now how it felt to have him holding her hand. She would never forget the strength that had flowed from his touch. That had been what had enabled her to pull herself together finally.

There was a warning bell sounding there. Trying to remind her that she'd once been totally dependent on someone else for that kind of strength and how hard it had been when it had been ripped away. But she didn't need to take heed, did she? She knew she had learned to rely on herself. A moment to take strength from someone else was excusable given that she had just come through major surgery and it wasn't as if Jack's intentions had been anything other than professional.

Even if there'd been the faintest possibility of there being anything else, seeing her looking such a mess would certainly have killed it. Not only that, he'd probably thought she was about to dissolve again at any moment. No wonder he'd been so pleased when Dr Kingsley had come into the room and they had been able to discuss purely medical matters. And that had been fine by her. She'd got to lie back with her eyes shut and let her mind drift on a wave of drug-induced peace with the added comfort of knowing she would be independent and brave again as soon as she had healed.

If she took a deep breath and let herself relax just a tiny bit more, she could slip into that new and improved fantasy that Jack would be starring in. Now that she knew who he was, the knowledge of how unwise that would be was perfectly clear despite the fuzziness of her thought processes but, somehow, it didn't seem to matter. The pull towards the fantasy was way too powerful, thanks to the sound of his voice, so close to her bed.

Of course it was Dr Kingsley who was pressing gently on her abdomen, but Lizzie didn't mind a bit that her skin was exposed to the other man present. She liked having Jack in the room. When this consultation was finished he would disappear, along with Dr Kingsley, and she might never see him again.

'Did that hurt?'

Lizzie forced her eyelids open as the words finally penetrated. From somewhere in the fuzziness in her head she caught the echo of the tiny groan she must have uttered aloud at the thought of never seeing Jack Rousseau again. Oh...*God*...

'Um...no. I don't think so.'

'Hmm.' Dave's voice faded as he turned to speak to someone else. The nurse, perhaps. 'We'll bump up the morphine in the IV. She's on PCA?'

'Yes,' the nurse confirmed.

Patient-controlled analgesia. She had a small remote and she could press the button if she wanted to increase the dose. With just a click, she could probably retreat into that very pleasant land of fantasy for hours to come. But if she did that, she wouldn't be seeing Misty until the drugs wore off. Lizzie curled her hands gently into fists.

Maybe someone else pushed the button. The voices faded completely and when she opened her eyes again, her room was empty of medical staff. To her joy, there were visitors she was desperate to see.

'Mum... Holly...hello, darling.'

'Hello, Mummy. Is your tummy sore?' Holly climbed carefully onto the end of the bed and hugged Lizzie's feet.

'No, it's fine.' Lizzie smiled at her daughter but instantly raised her gaze to her mother. 'How's Misty?'

'She's fine, too. Doing really well, they tell us.'

'They let me sit in the chair with Nanna,' Holly said proudly. ''Cos I told them I'd be really, really quiet. Like a little Christmas mouse.'

Lizzie was astonished. She gaped at her mother. 'They let Holly into the intensive care unit? I thought they'd be looking after her in the relatives' area while you were in there.'

'I think they made an exception because of the twin thing. Don't worry.' Maggie bent and gave Lizzie a kiss. 'She's so used to seeing Misty on dialysis, I don't think the equipment fazed her in the least.'

'Misty's asleep,' Holly told her. 'She won't wake up till tomorrow. And she's got this special bag on her bed. The nurse told me that when her new kidney starts working, that's where her wee is going to go.'

Lizzie's question was silent but Maggie shook her head. 'Not yet,' she said quietly. 'But the doctors are happy. They've both been up there, checking on every tiny detail. He's a nice young man, that Dr Jack of yours.'

'He's not *my* Dr Jack, Mum. He's not even my surgeon. He's just working with Dr Kingsley and making a film for his lectures. I'm sure we'll be delighted that he's here if anything goes wrong but he doesn't need to be nice. He just needs to be very, very good at his job.'

'Never hurts to be nice,' Maggie murmured.

Holly's eyes were wide as she listened to the exchange. 'Is Dr Jack being nice to you, too, Mummy?'

It was sweet how important it seemed to be. Lizzie smiled reassuringly. Dr Jack had given her fistfuls of tissues. He'd held her hand and made her smile. He'd taken very good care of Misty.

'Oh, yes,' she murmured. 'Very nice.'

But Holly wasn't listening any longer. She was leaning over the edge of Lizzie's bed.

'Ooh… You've got one of those special bags, too, and it's all full of yellow stuff. Is that your wee?'

'Mmm. I've got a thing called a catheter so I don't have to get up to go to the loo. They're going to take it out later.'

'When?'

'Soon, I hope. I want to go and visit Misty.'

Maggie looked horrified. 'You're not planning on getting out of that bed and walking for miles, I hope.'

Lizzie sighed. 'No, Mum. I thought they could wheel my bed over to the ICU.' Her voice wobbled and she pressed her lips together, willing the tears not to return. She would frighten Holly if she started crying again. She didn't want to upset her mother either. Maggie was looking very anxious. But why couldn't anybody understand?

'I just want to *see* her,' she whispered.

Her mother reached out to stroke her hair. 'I know, love. And it's hard but you've got to take care of yourself, too…for Misty's sake as well as the rest of us. She's fast asleep. She wouldn't even know if you were there.'

But *I'd* know, Lizzie thought stubbornly.

'Are you sure you're all right?' Maggie was looking close to tears herself. 'I could call your nurse. Or Dr Kingsley. Or that nice Dr Jack.'

Lizzie shook her head as firmly as she could. 'I'm fine, Mum. I feel a bit like I've been run over by a steamroller, that's all.' She gave her mother the best smile she could summon. Maggie had more than enough on her plate without having to worry about *her* state of mind. 'A good rest and I'll bounce back. I'll be able to go home by the end of the week.'

Maggie sniffed softly but nodded. 'That's what we want to hear,' she said brightly. 'That's where we're going now, isn't it, Holly? Home to have a bit of tea and feed Dougal. And then we'll pop back to say goodnight to you and Misty.'

Lizzie closed her eyes as she drew in a careful breath. 'Thanks, Mum. I really don't know what I'd do without you.'

'It's what mums are for.'

Lizzie opened her eyes. Her smile wobbled. 'You're the best of the lot. Not only are you taking care of me and the girls and all this hospital stuff, you've even found room for a hairy, smelly dog in your apartment.'

'Dougal doesn't smell.' Holly sounded offended.

'He might by now,' Maggie said dryly. 'He might have been shut inside all day if Kerry didn't get off work early. Come on, sweetheart. Let's go and see what he found to chew up today. You can choose the prettiest Christmas tree from all the ones we can see in the shop windows on the way home.'

Lizzie watched them leave, her mother limping more than usual, with a small girl clutching her hand. She couldn't keep the tears away then and they were still rolling down her cheeks when her nurse came back into the room.

'Oh, dear...what's happened?'

Lizzie shook her head, saying nothing. How could she begin to explain how hard life was at the moment? How much she loved her mother? How incredibly precious her children were?

How desperately she wanted to see for herself that Misty was all right?

The nurse's smile was sympathetic. 'It's a bit rough after surgery, isn't it? It's amazing how quickly people get over donating a kidney, though. A bit like a Caesarean, I guess. When there's a positive motive for doing something, it seems to make it easier somehow. Now…let's get that catheter out and when you feel like you need the loo, we'll see how you go on your feet.'

The urge to slip into sleep and forget about everything filled the room after the nurse had gone again and for quite some time Lizzie dozed. She couldn't fall into a really deep sleep, however, because something important was floating around her brain, being elusive.

Something her nurse had said.

But all she'd chatted about had been how busy they were. Two nurses had gone home sick with a bug that was doing the rounds and there was more than one patient who needed a lot of care. It was just as well she was doing so well. If she needed someone, she could just ring her bell, but otherwise it might be a while before anyone popped back to check on her.

Yes…that was it. She was on her own. She didn't have any real idea how much time had passed while she'd been drifting in and out of sleep and trying to remember what was important but surely her mother and Holly would still be away for some time?

The PICU wasn't that far away. Along the corridor and up two floors in the lift. If she took it very carefully, she could go and have a look and then come back to her bed and nobody would even know she'd been missing.

She could just imagine the look on Maggie's face. She could also see a disapproving frown on the remarkably clear image of Jack's face that appeared. There would be a box that needed the tick erased, wouldn't there? But they weren't here. And she wouldn't do it if it felt like it was going to do any real damage. She could just test out what she'd be like on her feet, couldn't she? After all, the nurse had said that's what they'd do later.

Moving very slowly and cautiously, Lizzie let her legs dangle over the side of the bed as she sat up. She held onto the bedside cabinet very carefully when she lowered herself to the floor. The flash of pain in her tummy subsided quite quickly and, surprisingly, Lizzie didn't feel as faint as she had expected. In fact, she felt quite strong.

It was easy enough to disconnect her IV. Lizzie smiled. She might not be able to work as a nurse any more but her training came in useful in all sorts of ways these days.

Taking a step was a bit more of a mission. Lizzie eyed the door of her room, which looked further away than it had when she'd been lying in bed. It was only a few steps, though. If she could manage that, then she'd know whether she had any chance of getting to the elevator at the end of the corridor. At least there was a rail that ran down the walls out there. That would help quite a lot.

Very slowly, she edged her way to the door. Bent over a little, with her hands supporting her stomach. It became easier rather than harder, which was a good sign. By the time Lizzie could look out and see if the corridor was clear, it wasn't hurting very much at all.

She looked towards the nurses' station first. The area was bright with red and green crepe paper streamers and the occasional huge paper bell but it was reassuringly empty of people. The staff was obviously all busy with other patients. She turned her head to scan the other end of the corridor.

And found herself looking at the solid figure of a man wearing theatre scrubs.

Her imagination had got it a bit wrong. The look on Jack Rousseau's face wasn't disapproving. It was more like he'd seen a whole herd of flying pigs.

'Where the *hell* do you think *you're* going?'

CHAPTER FOUR

Her face was a picture.

A mix of guilty child and determined rebel. There was something else in her eyes as well. A longing that was bordering on desperation. A plea that no man could have resisted.

Jack could feel it touching something very deep in his chest.

It made him want to gather her close and hold her. To protect her. It made him want to stand and fight by her side, whatever the threat might be. It certainly made him suck in a good lungful of air. He felt it escape in a resigned kind of sigh.

'You were planning to walk all the way to the PICU, weren't you?'

Eyebrows lifted so that they disappeared under the soft curls on her forehead. Small, white teeth captured a lower lip. Half of it, anyway. Lizzie had amazing lips. Full and soft and clearly designed for smiling.

Or kissing…

Jack shook his head, trying to disrupt the errant thought before it got caught irretrievably in his memory. 'Why didn't you ask a nurse to take you in a wheel-chair?'

'They're awfully busy,' Lizzie said quickly. 'I didn't want to add to the pressure for anyone.'

'Nothing to do with the fact that they would prob-ably have said no?' Jack asked dryly.

She caught his gaze and couldn't quite control the twitch of her lips.

'Mmm…'

How could anybody keep a stern face after that hint of mischief in the almost smile?

'Don't move,' he ordered. 'I'll be right back.'

He could have left a message for Dave that his pa-tient needed a stern talking to. He could have taken her arm and marched her back to her bed himself. He could have found a nurse to help with the ill-advised excur-sion. Instead, Jack found himself propelling a wheel-chair down the corridor a couple of minutes later, with Lizzie comfortably seated and now wrapped in a warm dressing gown.

'Are you sure you've got time for this?'

'Dave's still in Theatre, closing up on a liver trans-plant patient. We were both going to have another look in on Misty before going home. I said I'd go and check on her after I'd checked that *you* were obeying instruc-tions so that you would recuperate as fast as possible.'

He could only see the top of Lizzie's head but he could swear she was smiling. And why wouldn't she be? She was on her way to see her daughter. She was getting exactly what she'd wanted.

And deserved, too, damn it. That fighting spirit took

his breath away. Not only was she prepared to give up a body part with all the pain and fear that had to accompany the gesture, she had been ready to push herself to the nth degree just so she could get close enough to see for herself that her child was all right.

It took very little time to get Lizzie to where she wanted to be. Beside Misty's bed. Jack got the nurses to adjust the position of some of the monitoring equipment so that he could park the wheelchair at the head of the bed. As close to the unconscious child as possible.

'Oh….' Lizzie's hand traced the shape of the small head on the pillow with infinite tenderness. 'I'm here, darling. Mummy's here.'

Her hand trailed down, staying in contact with Misty's arm until it reached a small, still hand that peeped out from the bandaging that covered IV lines. Very carefully, Lizzie took hold of Misty's hand. She lifted it just a little, bending gingerly forward until she could touch the small fingers with her lips.

The air in this space felt curiously thick all of a sudden. Full of…

Love.

A kind of love that was outside anything Jack had ever experienced. As an adult or a child.

Pure.

So powerful it blew everything else away. It even sucked the oxygen out of the air. That would explain why it felt hard to take a decent breath. And why there was a curious ache behind his ribs.

If he hadn't failed in his marriage, would he have had children of his own by now? Could he have experi-

enced a touch of what he was feeling around him? He'd
never know. And while it was his choice and perfectly
acceptable, it was also…very sad.

'I'll leave you to it,' he said, his voice oddly gruff.
'One of the nurses will take you back to your room
when you get tired.'

Lizzie looked up.

'Thank you *so* much, Jack,' she whispered.

The smile that accompanied the soft words was astonishing. It matched the glow in her eyes. Soft and
tender and still full of the overflow of the love she was
giving her child. Instead of feeling as if he was looking
at a scene that he was in no way a part of, Jack could
feel himself being drawn in.

He could almost imagine what it would be like to be
one of the people Lizzie loved.

It was…utterly compelling.

Disturbingly so.

Jack turned away, only to find Lizzie's mother on
her way into the unit, leading Holly by the hand. The
older woman was looking very tired and she was limping badly but the smile that Jack received was very like
her daughter's. This had to be where Lizzie had inherited her determination and grit and the ability to love
with such generosity.

What an amazing little family. How lucky were these
two little girls?

Maggie had spotted Lizzie beside Misty's bed. She
clicked her tongue in dismay but Jack smiled at her.

'She has permission to be here. But only until she's
tired and then she'll be escorted back to her room.'

'Mummy!' Holly's cry was joyous.

'*Shhh*,' Maggie warned.

'*Mummy.*'

The word was a whisper but still loud enough to make the nursing staff smile. Holly let go of her grandmother's hand and ran to the wheelchair. Lizzie gathered her under her free arm. She was still holding Misty's hand on the other side. Maggie went towards them and touched the top of Lizzie's head in a gentle caress.

This time, Jack made it out of the unit but that last picture of the small family was imprinted on his brain. Linked physically by touch but far more significantly by a love that left him feeling strangely left out.

Bereft, even.

Worse, it was making him revisit aspects of his own life he had considered dealt with and buried. If he dwelled on it, he might even start having doubts and that could only lead to the possibility of his life seeming less satisfying. He'd spent years getting his life exactly the way he wanted it. He'd made the choice between his career and his marriage. Or rather the choice had been made for him.

Maybe all he needed to do was remember that it was his commitment to his work that had made his marriage such a miserable failure. His wife, Celine, had told him in no uncertain terms the extent to which he had failed as a husband because of that. Just before she'd hurled the Christmas roast turkey through the window as he was picking up his car keys to answer the call that he simply couldn't delay responding to.

Bad enough to fail as a husband. How much harder

would it have been if children had been involved? To fail as a father?

Yes. This was definitely the right direction to take in getting his head together again.

A hot shower in the locker rooms helped as well. So did changing out of the scrubs. Getting out of the hospital was the next logical step. Right away from any potential source of these disturbing thoughts and unwelcome memories he was getting. The paperwork and writing and emails could all wait until the morning.

But where to go? It was only 6:00 p.m. and he wasn't on call even though he'd told Dave to get in touch if he wanted to discuss any of his current patients, and all he needed for that was to have his phone within reach. He'd stayed in his town apartment last night but if he really wanted to get away, maybe he should do the hour or so drive to his 'real' London home.

The property he had inherited in one of the prestigious green belts comprised several acres with its own woods and stream and a rambling old house. It was always available, thanks to his housekeeper, Mrs Benny, but he rarely stayed there. He really should rent it out if he was going to keep the place for investment purposes but somehow that decision had been put on the back burner.

Had he, subconsciously, wondered if there might be a time in the future when he would change his mind about having a family of his own? They went together, didn't they? The big house and the vast garden for children to have adventures in. And that was probably the real explanation of why he'd kept the place at all. The only really happy memories he had of his own child-hood were rare jewels that had everything to do with this particular property.

Good grief, he should put it on the market and be done with it. In the meantime, it would certainly not be a good idea to be rattling around in it by himself given the current disturbances to his state of mind.

He would go and have dinner somewhere nice and head back to the inner-city apartment. His upmarket bachelor pad with its bedroom, bathroom, kitchenette and tiny balcony with the view that probably made it an even better investment than the country estate. Why was it that the prospect of a gourmet meal and then the modern comfort of the apartment was less than appeal-ing right now?

Maybe it was the seasonal vibe that would permeate anywhere he chose to go in the city. Decorations every-where and, worse, Christmas delicacies on every menu.

Or was it because he would be alone?

Well, that was easily remedied. In fact, the solution was right in front of Jack as he stepped out of the the-atre locker rooms to leave the hospital. Fate decreed that one of the more attractive scrub nurses who had been present during Lizzie's surgery that morning happened to be coming out of the door of the female locker rooms at precisely the same moment.

What was her name again?

Ah…yes. 'Tania…' Jack turned on his best smile. 'Heading home?'

'Unless I get a better offer.'

Tania had an exceptionally pretty smile. She was

young, in her mid-twenties maybe and she was in civ-
vies now, which were a pair of well-fitting jeans and a
T-shirt kind of top that advertised her generous curves.

Curves that would probably look fantastic in a red
and black striped bustier. The glimmer of interest in
finding out was welcome. This was the distraction he
needed. His downward glance at Tania's outfit had been
discreet and he raised his gaze before his smile had
begun to fade.

She had the colouring that went with her Irish accent. Dark hair, pale skin and blue eyes.

And in the second that Jack registered the colour of
her eyes, he knew that he wasn't about to provide the
better offer.

The blue was just wrong. Not dark enough or warm
enough or…*something* enough. The hair was too dark
and too straight and Tania was too young.

You want *company* for the *night*, a small voice muttered in the back of his mind, you're not looking for a
life partner.

But it was too late. The comparison was simply there
and instead of being a distraction, Tania might only
make things worse.

'Good luck with that,' he heard himself saying aloud.
'Me—I've got a mountain of paperwork that needs
some attention.'

It was true. It would be an excellent idea to get a
decent head start on those lecture notes to accompany
the video footage and thanks to any appetite for food or
women being effectively squashed, that was what Jack
decided to do. He shut himself in his new office space,

spent thirty minutes attending to his most urgent emails, left phone messages for three surgeons in other London hospitals he was to visit and did some last-minute editing on a paper on whole-bowel transplantation that was due for publication in *The Lancet*.

He put off reviewing the video footage of today's surgeries. It was fourteen hours since he'd arrived at this hospital today and he was weary enough to feel quite... normal. If he put off watching and thinking about Lizzie and/or Misty's surgical procedures, he might even manage to keep feeling like that.

It seemed to work, so he put it off the next day as well, which was easy to do because he had to spend a lot of time away from Westbridge Park visiting other London hospitals. He checked up on Misty's progress late that evening to find the little girl still in the paediatric intensive care unit and still well sedated. The new kidney hadn't started functioning yet but she was stable and there was nothing to set off any alarm bells.

He popped in on Lizzie as well. Just to update his records on both his patients. It added a nice, personal note to his lectures when he could deliver a detailed summary of post-surgical progress on the patients. She would probably be asleep, anyway.

She wasn't. Lizzie was propped up on her pillows, the reading light a soft glow beside her.

'I'm behaving,' she assured him. 'I'm in bed, see? I'll be asleep soon, honestly.'

He believed her. She looked as if he had already been asleep. Comfortable and a bit...rumpled. Her hair was a cloud of curls on the pillows and the sheet wasn't

pulled up far enough to hide the lace on the top of her
nightgown.

He really shouldn't have come to visit. Except, now
that he was here, the thought was more like how could
he have stayed away?

'Did you have a good day?'

'Excellent, thank you.' Lizzie's smile was joyous. 'I
had a shower by myself this morning and I walked as
far as the elevators and back and I've been to see Misty
three times.' It seemed like a cloud crossed her face as
her smile faded. 'She's…doing fine, isn't she?'

'Yes.' Jack smiled, hoping that it would bring the
glow back to Lizzie's face. It didn't. 'She's doing very
well,' he added.

Lizzie's voice had a small wobble. 'Why isn't my
kidney working for her yet?'

'It can take time for things to settle down. Be patient,
Lizzie.'

She was hanging onto his every word. He had the
power to make life that little bit better for her right now
and it was a good feeling.

No. Make that a *great* feeling.

'Sleep well.' Disconcertingly, he had to clear his
throat because his words had a rough edge to them.
'You might be pleasantly surprised by what tomorrow
will bring.'

Jack was in Dave Kingsley's company the next day
when they made a visit to the PICU. It was no surprise
to find the three generations of Misty's family clustered
quietly around her bed.

His own pleasant surprise at seeing Lizzie again so early in the day was easy to disguise because everybody here was delighted. The bag hanging beneath Misty's bed had a small quantity of liquid in it.

Liquid gold.

The kidney was starting to function.

Lizzie was well on the way to her own recovery. She had walked all the way here herself, she informed her surgeon.

'And I can go home tomorrow, can't I, Dr Kingsley?'

'Indeed you can, my dear.'

'But when Misty gets shifted to the ward, I'll be able to come in and stay with her?'

'We'll see about that.'

It was Maggie who spoke up. Lizzie's mother was looking very weary, Jack noticed. And no wonder. How often had she been back and forth to the hospital in the last three days? Coping with the pain of that bad hip? Looking after a lively six-year-old and worrying about her other granddaughter and her daughter?

It wasn't his problem.

Having to be absent from Westbridge Park and in an operating theatre on the other side of the city for the rest of that day was a good thing.

Passing Lizzie and her mother and Holly by chance the next day when Lizzie was clearly leaving the hospital was also a good thing. She was well enough to be discharged. She was heading back out into the world to get on with her own life.

Just as he was doing.

There was no real reason to keep tabs on Misty's

progress now that she had been transferred to the paediatric ward and was doing well so there was every
chance that this was the last time Jack would see Lizzie.

This was how it should be.

How it needed to be.

So why did he feel this odd sense of loss that was
enough of a kick in the guts to make him unable to find
any words to say in the first moments when he'd stopped
with the intention of saying *au revoir* and wishing her
well?

CHAPTER FIVE

THIS was it.

The moment to say goodbye to the man who'd sparked a fantasy she would have in her head for ever. Who had won her trust by keeping her daughter's secret and had won her heart by helping her through her lowest moment and making it possible for her to see and touch her precious child when she'd needed to so desperately.

Dr Jack Rousseau. The world-famous transplant surgeon she'd been lucky enough to have had involved in her life for a whole week.

She'd probably never see him again.

Because of hospital protocol, Lizzie was being ferried to the front door in a wheelchair. Her mother had stopped pushing the moment Jack had paused with the clear intention of saying something.

Except that he wasn't saying anything.

It was Maggie who spoke first, breaking what was on the point of becoming an awkward moment.

'Come on, Holly. Let's take the bag and make sure the taxi is waiting near the door. We don't want Mummy to have to stand outside and get cold.'

Lizzie suddenly felt embarrassed by the wheelchair. Or maybe it was the fact that she was having to look so far up to see Jack's face, as if she were only Holly's age and just as vulnerable.

'I don't need this thing any more,' she declared. 'Thank goodness.'

She took her feet off the metal plates and bent to fold them out of the way so that she could stand up.

'Here, let me.' Jack bent and flipped them up.

For a moment, their heads were very close together. It wouldn't have mattered except that Jack chose that moment to glance sideways and catch Lizzie's gaze.

She should have been watching his hands, not his face, but, for a heartbeat and then two, she was caught. Was she imagining an unspoken message? That it was a shame that this was goodbye but it was the way things had to be?

When he extended his hand to offer her assistance to get out of the wheelchair, Lizzie took it without hesitation. But the touch was brief. It felt brisk and professional.

No whisper there of any missed opportunities. She must have imagined what she'd thought she'd seen in his eyes.

'So…' Jack let go of her hand as soon as she was on her feet. 'You're going home.'

'Yes. I'll be back every day, though, to see Misty.'

'I hear she's doing very well.'

'Yes.' Lizzie's smile came easily. 'She is. Another week and we'll have her home. In time for Christmas.'

Jack was giving her a smile that she would be happy

to see every day of her life. It was gorgeous. 'I hope it's the best Christmas ever. For all of you.'

'It will be.' The words were a vow. 'I...hope you have a wonderful Christmas, too, Jack.'

His smile faded. The warmth in his face seemed to fade as well and Lizzie had the odd impression that she'd said something wrong. Stepped over a boundary, perhaps, by saying something a little too personal to a member of staff?

He knew so much about her but what did she know about him? Virtually nothing. Why would she?

This moment could have become even more awkward than when he'd stopped in the first place but Maggie came back through the electronic doors.

'Taxi's here, love. We're all ready for you.' She smiled brightly at Jack. 'Thank you so much for everything you've done, Dr Rousseau.'

Still he seemed to hesitate.

'Will you be all right?' he asked. He gave Maggie a quick sideways glance and then straightened his stance. Even his tone was stiff. 'To get out to the taxi, I mean?'

It was Maggie who answered. 'We'll be fine,' she assured him. 'Thank you again, but we've taken up enough of your time. You must be a very busy man.'

'Indeed.' Jack merely raised a hand in farewell as Maggie took Lizzie's arm and walked with her to the doors.

Lizzie couldn't help a final, backward glance when was settled into the back seat of the taxi and they were pulling away from the hospital entrance.

Jack can't have been that busy, she thought, if he was only just moving away now.

Maggie insisted that Lizzie stayed at home and rest the next day but the day after that there was no stopping her from spending time with Misty. They all went in the afternoon and stayed until the evening, when Lizzie had to admit she was sore and tired and needed to go home.

The weather had turned bleak over the last couple of days. It was cold and wet with intermittent sleet and taxis were getting harder to find. That was probably why Maggie raced ahead of Lizzie as they came out of the hospital entrance that night. And why she slipped on the puddle of sleet and went crashing to the pavement.

'Oh, my God!' Lizzie ignored the stab of pain in her side as she rushed to where her mother had fallen and crouched beside her.

'*Mum*. Can you hear me?'

'Of course I can. I'm not deaf. Don't shout, love. Help me up.'

Lizzie started to but even in the artificial light muffled by another shower of sleet she could see the way the colour drained from Maggie's face. She could hear the stifled cry of pain. Holly burst into tears beside her.

Help arrived. A taxi driver leapt from his vehicle and then took off into the hospital. Staff from the emergency department arrived a commendably short time after that.

'Look at that,' a young doctor said. 'External rotation on her left foot. Visible shortening, too.'

'Fractured neck of femur?' someone else asked.

'I'd say so. Bring that stretcher over here. Let's get her inside.'

All Lizzie could do was to comfort Holly and wait after Maggie was taken to the emergency department. There was a wait for X-rays to be taken and an even longer wait for an orthopaedic surgeon to arrive for a consultation.

The surgeon was only in the department for a matter of minutes and he was a very cheerful man.

'No more waiting list for you, Mrs Donaldson. You'll get your new hip first thing tomorrow morning.'

After that, things became rather surreal for Lizzie. Her mother was transferred to the orthopaedic ward and had enough pain relief on board to be remarkably comfortable. Having promised to be back to see her before she got taken to Theatre in the morning, Lizzie made her way slowly down to the front door again with Holly.

Having reached the hospital foyer, she was intercepted by a young woman who turned out to be a social worker from the emergency department.

'I got sent to find you, Mrs Matthews. Thank goodness you hadn't left yet. I've heard that you're only just out of hospital yourself. Do you need help?'

Lizzie blinked at her. She still hadn't quite got her head around this new development. Her own exhaustion had been compounded by fear for her mother and the need to reassure Holly that the world wasn't really falling apart around them. All she'd been doing since the moment Maggie had fallen had been to cope with each moment as it came. Going home was the logical thing to do next and she'd been on her way until this perky young woman with a clipboard had stopped them.

'All I need is a taxi,' she said. 'So that we can get home.'

'Are you sure? How are you going to cope on your own with a child? We have foster-families available for just this kind of situation, you know.'

Lizzie tightened her grip around Holly's hand. 'That won't be necessary.'

'If you don't mind me saying so, Mrs Matthews, you don't look very well. What was it that you were in hospital for?'

'That really isn't any of your business.' Lizzie started moving again.

'Oh…I'm sorry, but it kind of is.' The social worker was following her. 'There's quite a difference in being able to look after yourself and having to look after someone else as well.'

Lizzie was almost at the door now. The social worker actually caught hold of her arm.

'And what about when your mother gets discharged? You're certainly going to need some help then, aren't you? We have all sorts of agencies that we can call on. We just need to fill in a few forms.'

'We'll be fine,' Lizzie said wearily. Aware of someone behind her, she stepped to one side so she wasn't blocking someone's exit. Except that the person didn't take the invitation to pass. He stopped. And stared.

'Lizzie…is everything all right?' Jack Rousseau asked. 'You know Mrs Matthews?' There was a look of relief on the face of the earnest young woman with the clipboard.

'Yes.' The response was cautious. It didn't take a genius to see that there was something very wrong here.

Lizzie's face was pale and tight and Holly looked just as miserable.

It had been two days since he'd said goodbye to her. He'd stood almost in the same place he was now and watched her exit from his life, with an echo of the feeling he'd had that day in the intensive care unit when he'd felt himself being drawn in to something he wasn't entitled to.

Finally forcing himself to turn and walk back into his own life, Jack could have sworn he'd felt something tear deep inside but the momentary pain had been quickly followed by a wave of…relief. He didn't have to even think about disturbing, personal issues any more. He'd thrown himself into the series of lectures that had kept him fully occupied for these two days and it had been exactly what he'd needed.

The harder he worked, the better. That way, he didn't have time to think about anything else.

Or anyone else.

That was why he hadn't hesitated in responding to that late call from Dave for a consult on his MVA patient with the kidney they were still trying to save. Which was why he was only just getting away from the hospital now, at 8:00 p.m.

'Nanna fell over.' It was Holly who spoke up. 'She has to have a hopper-shun.'

'Operation,' Lizzie murmured. She met Jack's gaze. 'Mum slipped on an icy patch outside and broke her hip. The surgery's scheduled for tomorrow morning.'

'And Mrs Matthews is only just out of hospital herself,' the social worker put in. 'There's some concern about her being able to manage.'

'I'm not about to let Holly go and stay with strangers.' Lizzie's tone was clipped. 'Thanks, anyway, but we'll manage just fine.'

Would they? Lizzie's independence was admirable but was she overestimating her capabilities? He couldn't simply take her word for it and walk away feeling relieved that he didn't need to get involved again. He couldn't let some social worker try and take Holly away from her mother either.

'Do you have anyone else that could help? A relative or friend?'

Lizzie nodded. 'There's Kerry. She lives in the flat next door and she's been helping out with Dougal.'

'Dougal?' Jack could feel his eyes widen. There was a man involved here as well? And what if there was? It shouldn't make him feel… Good grief…it couldn't possibly be a touch of jealousy, could it?

'Dougal's our puppy.' Holly's voice was muffled because her face was pressed against her mother's leg.

'A two-year-old bearded collie,' Lizzie amended. Her smile was wry. 'Puppy is a more accurate description, though. He still bounces and chews everything.'

'And this Kerry is looking after him?' This sounded hopeful. Anyone who could care for a dog would probably be good with small children.

'She lets him out if we're away for a long time. But…'

'Kerry's fat,' Holly informed Jack. 'She's going to have a baby.'

'And she's still working,' Lizzie said. 'She's a barmaid at the pub down the road. But I don't *think* she's working tonight. She'll be happy to help. *If* it's needed.'

The young social worker was looking doubtful.

Jack knew he shouldn't look at Lizzie. This was none of his business. He should excuse himself and let the system do what it was there to do. But he couldn't help himself.

'All we need is a taxi,' Lizzie was saying.

She sounded calm enough but Jack could see she was almost at breaking point. Close to tears, probably, because there was an odd sheen to her eyes that made them appear even bluer than ever.

How many blue-eyed women had he known or had yet to meet? How could he possibly be this certain that only one pair of eyes could ever be this perfect colour? Or could make him feel like he could bend or break any rules and get away with it? That he wanted to, because if he did, somehow it would make the world a better place.

For Lizzie.

And for himself.

'There's no need for a taxi,' he heard himself saying. 'I'm heading home myself. I'll give you both a lift.'

CHAPTER SIX

'IF YOU park here, your car should be safe for a while.'

Lizzie crossed her fingers in her lap. How bizarre was it to be rolling up to a housing estate like this, cushioned on the leather upholstery of a sleek, late-model BMW?

'That light isn't broken again yet,' she added, 'and Mr Stubbs lives in a ground-floor apartment and spends his life watching what happens outside his window. It's that one, with the reindeer, see?'

Nobody could miss spotting that window. The reindeer were made of lurid red and green lights that flashed on and off. Two standing reindeer and a leaping one in the middle, all pulling sleighs. They flashed in sequence to give the impression of movement.

Illuminated by the deer, a curtain twitched reassuringly as Jack killed the engine and got out of the driver's seat. She waved in the direction of the window and then turned to see Jack looking upwards. She could understand where that grim expression was coming from. She'd been shocked herself at the first sight of this tenement block but that had been long ago, before she'd got to know some of the people who lived on her mother's floor. Good people lived here, amongst a few less desirable neighbours, and they made up for the tough living conditions.

One day, maybe, when they'd got through this rough patch of their lives and she could return to a full-time job, she'd be able to afford to move her little family somewhere else. Something semi-detached in a suburb would be perfect. Kerry was trying to talk her into emigrating to New Zealand but that was a bit too much of a fantasy for now.

In the meantime, Lizzie had to get past the embarrassment of the rubbish littering the grey, tiled flooring and the dim glow from unadorned light bulbs in the entranceway. She had to introduce Jack to Kerry, convince him that she could manage and then send him back to the world of being a famous surgeon and driving the kind of car that was probably worth at least two years of the rent she would have to pay to live in her dream house.

Please be home, Kerry, she prayed, waiting for what seemed an interminable length of time for the lift to come down.

'What floor are you on?' Jack's voice was so controlled it was devoid of expression.

'Ten,' Holly piped up. 'I can reach the button.' She stood on tiptoe and stretched. 'See?'

'Good girl.'

Holly beamed but Jack was staring straight ahead. Watching the doors slide shut and no doubt reading some of the obscenities scratched deeply into the metal or inked with indelible pen. Machinery screeched and clanged and the ancient lift jerked its way up.

'We usually take the stairs,' Lizzie muttered into the uncomfortable silence. 'It's good exercise.'

'Nanna doesn't, though,' Holly said. ''Cos she's got a funny leg.' She pressed against her mother. 'But they're going to fix it now, aren't they, Mummy? That's why she has to stay in the host-hostible, isn't it?'

'Hospital,' Lizzie murmured automatically. 'Mmm.'

She stroked Holly's curls. That's where she should be at the moment, by her mother's side, keeping her company and providing reassurance about tomorrow's surgery.

Or with her other daughter, speeding her recovery with her willpower and sheer determination that life was going to get better for them all.

But she needed to be here with Holly as well.

It felt like she was pulled in different directions with so much force it was threatening to tear her apart.

She was sore. And tired.

Thank goodness Kerry was home.

'Gidday.' Her neighbour was wearing a Santa hat and she grinned down at Holly, who had insisted on being the one to knock on the door that led to the shared balcony on the edge of the tenement building. Kerry held her arms out instantly, looking up as Holly gladly accepted the hug, her small arms only getting part of way around an impressively swollen belly. Then she looked up and saw Lizzie's face.

'Lizzie! What's wrong? Where's Maggie?'

Her gaze shifted and her jaw visibly dropped as she caught sight of Jack, standing back a little and looking tall and dark and more than a little dangerous in the shadows.

The sideways glance from Lizzie showed her that he was returning the gobsmacked stare. Some people couldn't get past their first impression of Kerry with the numerous bits of silverware adorning her ears and eyebrows and nostrils and even underneath her bottom lip. At least the hat was hiding the startling fluorescent pink streaks she had in her hair but if you added the fact that she was only eighteen, single and about to produce her own child to the initial impression, Jack would probably be inclined to call in social services himself.

'Slight complication,' Lizzie said to Kerry, gathering her strength. 'Nothing we can't handle, though, with a bit of help from you.'

'You've got it, mate.' Kerry spoke without hesitation. 'What can I do?'

This was beyond belief.

Jack actually winced as the door to Maggie's apartment was opened and a large, hairy creature bounded out joyously and leapt at him.

'Dougal!' Holly was trying to sound authoritative. '*Bad* dog.'

He could swear the dog was laughing. A claw dug painfully into his thigh as the animal pushed off to launch itself towards the small girl. Holly was unperturbed. She was hugging Dougal as she lost her balance and tumbled into a sitting position.

Good grief! As if it wasn't unhygienic enough to be having her face licked by a dog, the floor of this shared balcony was probably indescribably filthy. Lizzie was flicking on a light now and he got another glimpse of her neighbour's extraordinary hair and the glimmer of all the hardware of her facial piercings.

This place was a circus.

Housed in a high-rise slum.

No way should Lizzie be allowed to stay here in her condition. She'd pick up some ghastly infection and probably die and then what would happen to her mother and those two little girls who wanted a daddy for Christmas?

'Thank you very much for the lift home,' Lizzie said, standing back to let Kerry past. 'We'll be fine now.'

Jack's doubts must have been written all over his face because Lizzie bit her lip.

'Come in for a bit,' she invited. 'And see for yourself. I'll make a cup of tea.'

'In your dreams,' Kerry said cheerfully. 'You're going to be putting your feet up. The kitchen's out of bounds except for me and Prickles, here.'

'Prickles?' Jack echoed faintly.

Holly was scrambling to her feet using one of the dog's ears for balance. 'That's *me*,' she informed him. 'Cos Kerry says that holly has prickles.'

'Like a hedgehog.' Kerry grinned over her shoulder. 'And everybody knows that I *love* hedgehogs.'

Jack followed the small procession into the apartment and pushed the front door closed behind him.

Something odd happened as the door clicked shut. Almost instantly, the grim, grey world outside seemed to vanish. This apartment was as clean and bright as a brand-new penny. There was a fresh scent of something flowery that was only faintly dampened by a more canine odour. And it was full of colour. Bright rugs on

the floor and cushions like big, fat jewels on the couch
and chairs. Children's artwork was proudly displayed
on the walls, along with dozens of photographs, and
there was even a jam jar with fresh flowers in it on the
table. The contrast to what lay on the other side of the
door made these small rooms feel warm and cosy and
welcoming.

'Park yourself there,' Kerry ordered Lizzie, waving
at the couch. 'Dougal...cut it *out*.'

The dog dropped to the floor with his nose on his
front paws. A contrite, doggy pancake with a tail that
obviously couldn't stay still.

Lizzie lowered herself slowly onto the couch. 'Please
sit down,' she invited Jack. 'Kerry won't let you go until
you've had a cup of tea and a bikkie.'

Kerry was moving with surprising speed for someone in the late stages of pregnancy. She disappeared
into another room and came back seconds later with
her arms full of pillows and a patchwork quilt, insisting
that Lizzie get tucked up on the couch like a pampered
invalid. Then she busied herself in the tiny, adjoining
kitchen. It couldn't be easy manoeuvring herself in that
space with both Holly and the dog in the way but the
strange-looking girl seemed to be blessed with endless
patience.

'Don't climb on the bench, Prickles. Use the stool to
get into the cupboard... Here...I'll help.'

At the same time as supervising her helper, Kerry
was chatting to Lizzie and finding out about Maggie's
accident.

'I'll take the day off work tomorrow,' she announced
as soon as she was satisfied Maggie was being well

looked after. 'I can look after Holly while you're with your mum. Yeah…OK, Prickles. I reckon we'll go for the chocolate bikkies but only cos we've got a visitor.'

He was the visitor. He didn't belong here and Jack had the uncomfortable feeling that he was spying on something that was none of his business. Looking for reasons why it wasn't a suitable space for a patient who should rightly be still safely tucked up in a hospital bed.

It would be easy to find something to criticise. The place wasn't that tidy. There were toys strewn about and a dog bed in the corner that harboured some disgusting, well-chewed items. But it was just as easy to ignore such details. This was so far away from anything Jack had ever been familiar with and yet he recognised it.

This was what a home was like.

Lizzie would be fine. She was in the place she belonged and with the people she loved. People that loved her and would care for her.

He could leave.

Except that now he had a mug of tea in his hand and Holly was offering him a plate of chocolate biscuits with palpable pride.

'They're *squiggle tops*,' she whispered loudly.

Kerry saw the way he eyed the slightly lurid decorations on the biscuits. 'My mum sends them from New Zealand,' she told him. 'They're not half-bad, though.'

'They're the best bikkies in the world,' Holly assured him. 'Kerry's going to send them to me when she goes home.'

'You're going home?' It was crazy, but Jack couldn't help honing in on a potential reason to continue worrying about Lizzie. 'When?'

'After bubs here makes an appearance. I left it a bit late to book a flight.'

'Lucky for us.' Lizzie shook her head, refusing anything to eat. She looked pale and very tired. 'Holly, it's time you were in bed, hon.'

'Sure is,' Kerry agreed. 'Come on, let's get those jim-jams on. And you'll have to go to sleep really fast.'

'Why?' Both Holly and Dougal were following Kerry from the room.

'Because I'm going to sleep in Misty's bed and that way you won't hear me snoring.'

Jack caught Lizzie's gaze as they heard Holly's giggle. They both smiled and suddenly it was hard to look away. The joy in that sound was enough to make his throat feel oddly tight. These people might have very little in terms of material wealth but they had something that was priceless. This atmosphere of a home and family, however different, meant that moments of happiness could be conjured up like magic.

It seemed like an extension of that magic that Lizzie knew exactly what he was feeling. He could see it reflected in those amazing blue eyes and it took an astonishing effort to break the contact. He ate his odd biscuit hurriedly, washing it down with tea that was hot enough to scald his throat.

'I'd better be going.' He shook his head as Lizzie started pushing back the quilt covering her. 'No, don't get up. If you're planning on being back at Westbridge tomorrow, you need all the rest you can get.'

'I'll rest.'

'She absolutely will,' Kerry assured him, appearing

again with Holly holding her hand and looking smaller, somehow, in her pink pyjamas. 'Here, I'll see you out.'

She opened the door and Jack stepped out into the greyness he'd virtually forgotten about. For an insane moment, he wanted to turn around and go back into that bright apartment. Maybe it was just as well the door was shutting behind him. He needed to take a deep breath before he moved, though, and in that momentary hesitation there came a loud sound like a muffled explosion from somewhere on a lower floor. The door behind him flew open again.

'What on earth was that?' Kerry marched to the edge of the balcony and peered down.

Jack was beside her. They could see people running away from the building they were in. Moments later they heard the first sirens.

'Holy cow...' Kerry breathed. 'I can see smoke!'

The explosion had been enough to rock the couch Lizzie was lying on.

Her eyes had been drifting shut, her mind still full of the extraordinary reality of Dr Jack Rousseau sitting here in this apartment only a minute ago. Of that moment he'd looked at her when they'd heard the delicious sound of Holly's giggle. Of seeing something almost like yearning in that dark gaze that had captured her heart and squeezed it hard.

She came completely awake with painful swiftness to hear Kerry's shocked cry about the smoke. And then alarms began ringing throughout the building. Her heart started thumping wildly and she pushed herself up so fast her head spun. She could see stars and hear buzzing sounds around her that were receding and then coming back like waves.

'Just relax,' came a clearer voice. 'I've got you.'

Lizzie could feel the quilt tighten around her body like a cocoon. She could feel the immense strength in the arms that were picking her up as if she were no more than Holly's size. The desire to simply relax into that hold and lay her head on a broad shoulder was over-whelming but she fought back.

'Holly...'

'Kerry's got her. And Dougal.'

'Is there a fire?'

'We don't know. We're getting out just in case.'

The alarms were louder now and there were many other voices. Frightened adults asking what was going on. Crying children. Jack's voice rumbled in his chest so that Lizzie could feel as well as hear it.

'Nobody use the lifts. Take the stairs.'

Ten floors of concrete stairs with a press of semi-panicked people. The jolts were painful but it was far worse not to be able to see and hold Holly.

'Hang onto me,' she heard Jack say. 'Holly, don't let go of Kerry's hand, OK?'

'OK, Dr Jack.'

The courage in that small voice brought a lump to Lizzie's throat that made it hard to drag in her next breath. Even harder not to let it go in a sob. To her dis-belief, she felt the press of Jack's cheek against her hair and his voice was close enough to tickle her ear.

'We're almost there, Lizzie. Hang on. Everything's under control.'

For a blissful moment, Lizzie let herself believe that. She could let herself feel protected.

Safe.

And then she felt the curl of smoke in her nostrils and the bite of the icy night air on her face. She could see the flash of beacons from emergency vehicles and hear the sounds of shouted directions and the hum of an increasingly anxious crowd.

Under control? Her life seemed to be one disaster after another.

'That's your car?' she heard someone yell.

'Yes.'

'Move it now. We need more space for emergency vehicles.'

'Sure.'

Lizzie found herself gently lowered into the front passenger seat. She heard a back door open.

'Hop in, Holly,' Kerry ordered.

'But what about Dougal?'

Turning her head, Lizzie could see that Holly had a firm hold on Dougal's lead. Dougal had his favourite possession—a well-chewed stuffed toy duck—clamped in his jaws. For once, the dog's tail wasn't wagging.

'Get this car moved,' someone yelled. *'Now.'*

'Get in.' Jack sounded resigned. 'Dougal too.'

The car bounced as the back seat filled up. Jack slid into the driver's seat, started the engine and drove to where a police officer was signalling. He parked the car, leaving the engine going to run the heater, and for a long while they sat there watching the activity around the tenement building. Holly fell asleep on Kerry's lap. Dougal's anxious huffing steamed up the windows.

'I can't see any flames,' Kerry ventured. 'I'll bet it was only a small fire. Maybe Mr Stubbs blew something up in his microwave. They'll probably let us back in soon.'

'I'll go and find out.' Jack got out of the car, turning his coat collar up against the flurries of sleet. He got as far as the bright tape that was preventing anyone from going back inside. They could see him having a conversation with a senior-looking policeman.

When he came back, he simply sat, with his hands on the steering-wheel, staring through the windscreen.

Lizzie's heart sank. 'What?' she whispered. 'What's wrong?'

'There was methamphetamine in the building,' Jack said slowly. 'It blew up. Apparently nobody's been hurt but they're worried about contamination. Nobody's going to be allowed back in tonight. Maybe not for several days. They're setting up some kind of emergency accommodation in a church hall around here somewhere.'

The silence when he'd finished speaking grew as the implications sank in. Lizzie was in no condition to be in a temporary shelter with hundreds of other people.

'We could go to the pub where I work,' Kerry offered into the silence. 'They might be able to give us a room of our own.'

'Good idea.' Lizzie tried hard to sound enthusiastic but a wobble in her voice betrayed her. Jack turned his head.

'No,' he said. 'It's not a good idea.'

Another silence fell and then Jack spoke again. Decisively.

'Put your safety belts on,' he ordered. He waited until they complied and then eased the car through a gap between a fire engine and a police car.

'Is Holly properly buckled in?'

'Yes.' Kerry sounded unusually subdued.

'Where are we going?' Lizzie ventured.

'Somewhere you'll all be safe,' was all Jack said.

It was the logical thing to do.

For heaven's sake, he had this barn of a house that he rarely even visited but that his housekeeper, Mrs Benny, took pride in keeping ready for instant use. There would be fresh linen in at least eight bedrooms and clean towels in the bathrooms. The fridge and larder would be well stocked and if they weren't, that could be easily remedied in the morning.

Mrs Benny was astounded by the late-night phone call.

'Visitors? At this time of night? How many visitors?'

'Three,' Jack said, and then thought of what might happen when Maggie was released from hospital. 'At the moment,' he added.

He heard a sniff on the other end of the line.

'And a dog,' he said.

The appalled silence was annoying. He could see the problem, of course. His housekeeper had had the house virtually to herself for years now and it was always the same. Perfectly polished and nothing even an inch out of place. Sterile.

His housekeeper probably thought he was out of his mind. She could be correct but the fact that somebody else might think so was galvanising somehow.

Right from the moment he'd seen Maggie lying on the ground outside the hospital he'd had a gnawing anxiety about how Lizzie was going to cope. Now that he'd been handed the opportunity to assist in a practical way, that knot of tension was going away.

And it felt…good.

'Never mind, Mrs Benny,' he said crisply. 'We can manage without you tonight. Sorry to have disturbed you.'

It meant the house was dark and chilly when they finally arrived but Jack could deal with that. He flicked every light switch he went past and cranked up the central heating to maximum.

'Whose house is this?' Lizzie asked in a dazed voice.

'Mine.'

'You…you *live* here?'

'No. It's empty. And available. Come upstairs and you can choose the rooms you'd like to use. Kerry, do you think you can find your way around the kitchen and look after the others?'

'No worries, Dr Rousseau.'

They put Lizzie in a spacious bedroom that had an en suite bathroom. Holly chose the room next door and Kerry would be on the other side of the hallway. Kerry's eyes had been getting steadily wider as Jack showed them around the house.

'This is a palace,' she said in awed tones.

'What's a palace?' Holly's words were distorted by a huge yawn.

'Where a princess lives,' Kerry told her.

'Am I a princess?'

'For tonight you are. Princess Prickles.'

Holly yawned again.

'Bedtime,' Kerry decreed. 'Come on, we'll go and give Mummy a kiss and then you can go to sleep.'

There was no reason for Jack to follow them on the mission but he found himself doing so, with Dougal plodding beside him.

'Ni' night Mummy,' Holly said. 'Sleep tight. Don't let the bed bugs bite.'

Jack's lips twitched. Imagine if Mrs Benny had heard that?

He left them to get settled and went back downstairs, heading for the drawing room and the crystal decanter that would be full to the brim with a vintage bourbon. It wasn't until he'd poured himself a glass and was standing beside the multi-paned French doors looking into a garden that was too dark to see that he realised he wasn't alone.

For some obscure reason, Dougal had followed him downstairs. He was sitting there quietly, the toy duck lying on the floor in front of him, and when Jack looked at him, he lifted his ears and wagged his tail.

'Oh... I guess you need to go outside?'

The tail wagged harder. It took a few moments to figure out how to unlock the French doors and Jack felt obliged to step outside himself as well. It would be a disaster if the beloved family pet took off and disappeared, wouldn't it?

There was a thin covering of snow on the expanse of lawn that Dougal seemed to find incredibly exciting. He put his nose into the snow and ran in circles, ploughing up flakes that were soon stuck all over his shaggy coat.

Jack took another swallow of his bourbon to try and keep the cold at bay. He'd never owned a dog but he remembered wanting one desperately when he'd been a boy.

Especially when he'd stayed here with his mother. The upper-floor apartment he'd shared with his father in Paris most of the time had been no more suitable for keeping pets than the tenement block Dougal was currently living in. But here…there were acres of garden and a small forest and a stream and even as a child he'd known that paradise could have been enhanced by having the faithful companionship of a dog.

Memories of this place were bitter-sweet. The visits had been few and far between. Random acts of duty from a mother who had been too busy living her glamorous life. A break from the greyness of the life he'd had with a father who had never recovered from the blow of his wife leaving and had buried himself in his work ever since.

He would have felt important if he'd owned a dog. Needed, maybe.

Wanted.

Jack drained the last of his bourbon. 'Come on,' he ordered the dog. 'Inside.'

Kerry came into the drawing room as he fastened the doors again.

'Can I make you a coffee or anything?' she asked.

'No, thanks. I'll head back into the city. If you think you can manage?'

'We'll manage fine.' Kerry's serious expression made her look older than her years. 'Why are you doing this for us, Dr Rousseau?'

'It's nearly Christmas,' was the best he could come up with. 'And…um…call me Jack.' He rattled his car keys in his pocket and started for the door.

Kerry followed him. 'Where are we exactly? Only I'll need to send for a taxi or something in the morning so that Lizzie can get in to see her mum.'

'No need. I'll have a car and driver sent out. Will you be all right here with Holly for the day?'

'Are you kidding? This is like winning some luxury holiday or something.'

'Good.' Jack was at the front door. 'I've left my card by the phone. Call me on my mobile if you're worried about anything.'

'OK.' Kerry was silent as he went outside but then she called out softly. 'Hey…Jack?'

He turned around. 'Yes?'

'I guess people tell you all the time but you're a really nice guy.'

No. Jack thought about that as he walked to his car. Nobody had ever told him that exactly.

It brought a disturbing echo of a small girl's voice into his mind.

He has to be nice…and kind…and he has to be really, really nice to Mummy so she'll like him too…

Oh…*mon Dieu*…what *was* he doing?

CHAPTER SEVEN

'It was like something out of a movie, Mum. A car and a *chauffeur*. Can you believe it?'

'He's such a *nice* man, your Jack.'

'He's not my Jack, Mum.'

But Lizzie let her eyes drift shut for a heartbeat's wishful thinking. Jack Rousseau was, without doubt, the most astonishing man she'd ever met and he had been unbelievably kind in the face of her family's adversity, but what man in his right mind would be interested in *her*?

Not only was she minus a kidney and pathetically weak herself right now, she had a sick child and a mother who was about to be taken to Theatre to get a new hip.

Crazy.

Her whole world was crazy at the moment.

'I'm sorry about the apartment, Mum. I have no idea what's going to happen. I'll make some enquiries today and at least see if I get can some clothes and things out for us.'

'I'll be here for a few days anyway, darling. I'm sure things will be sorted by then.' Maggie's eyes were drifting shut thanks to the level of pain relief she'd been given. 'How's Misty?'

'I'm going to go and see her while you're in Theatre.'

'I'm sorry…' Maggie's voice trembled. 'I've caused you extra worry.'

Lizzie squeezed her hand. 'It's a blessing in disguise, if you ask me. OK, the timing wasn't the best but you're getting a new hip. You won't be languishing on a waiting list for goodness knows how long. It's the best Christmas present you could ask for, really.'

'But how are *you*?'

'Fine. Just…tired.'

More like she'd had the stuffing completely knocked out of her but Maggie didn't need to hear that. Fortunately she was too drowsy to notice how much of an effort it was for Lizzie to walk alongside the bed as she was taken away for surgery. Or that she got horribly dizzy when she bent to kiss her mother.

'Are you OK?' the orderly asked.

Lizzie nodded, giving Maggie's hand a final squeeze. 'I'll be in to see you as soon as they let me. I love you.'

Maggie's words were a little slurred. 'Give Misty a kiss from Nanna.'

'I will.'

To her joy, Misty was awake enough to return the kiss. And she was smiling. The PICU nurse told Lizzie that permission might be given to transfer her to the children's ward today. Dr Kingsley was going to decide when he did his rounds.

Dr Kingsley had more than the company of his junior doctors on his rounds. Lizzie felt her heart rate pick up and the bone-numbing fatigue ebb noticeably when Jack smiled at her. Good grief…the man only had to be breathing the same air as she was and the world seemed a much brighter place. She was dangerously close to falling head over heels in love with him.

Dave was more than happy with Misty's progress but he frowned noticeably when he took a second look at Lizzie.

'You need to be properly checked out. Don't you think, Jack?'

'I do indeed.'

The concern in that rich voice nearly undid Lizzie. It curled inside her, creating a melting warmth and a yearning that was overwhelming. It whispered the heady suggestion that he really did care about her.

And how on earth was she going to convince herself that he had no interest in being more than a good Christmas elf when he sounded like that? And looked at her like that? When she was now staying in his house, for heaven's sake?

'You haven't exactly been following orders and getting the rest you need, have you?' Dave asked.

'I haven't really had a choice.'

Her doctor sighed. 'So I heard. Jack filled me in on what happened to your mother. How's she doing?'

'I'm about to go and find out.' Had Jack not said anything about her apartment crisis? About putting them up in his house for the night? Why not? Was he embarrassed about a less than professional involvement with a colleague's patient? Or was he simply doing a good deed that meant nothing more and wasn't worth mentioning? Yes, that was probably it.

Lizzie hitched in a breath. 'She should be out of Theatre by now.'

'Don't you walk up there,' Dave commanded. 'And I want to see you in the ward as soon as you've made your visit. I'm going to run a few tests on you, my dear, and if you don't pass, you might find yourself back in here overnight.'

'But—' It was only that she was tired. Worrying about her mother had meant she hadn't slept at all last night.

'No buts.' Dave Kingsley was looking stern. 'And I meant what I said about not walking around the hospital at the moment. You look like a breath of wind would blow you over. We'll find a wheelchair and someone to push it.'

'Someone who'll make sure you get delivered to the surgical ward afterwards for that check-up,' Jack added.

Dave smiled. 'Good thinking. Needs to be someone she won't be able to wrap around her little finger as well. You want to volunteer?'

Jack's expression was unreadable. 'It would be my pleasure.'

Some of the expressions on the faces of the other medical staff waiting for Dr Kingsley to finish his patient's visit were far more readable. A junior female doctor nudged her friend and sent a ghost of a wink in Lizzie's direction.

She hoped, fervently, that Jack hadn't seen it.

The first opportunity to say anything at all to him didn't come until she found herself being propelled along a hospital corridor, minutes later.

'This is getting to be a habit,' she muttered. 'Sorry for taking up so much of your time.'

'Not a problem.' Jack's voice was well above her head level and sounded kind of distant. 'There was no real reason for me to finish rounds with Dave and I've got a lecture at Hammersmith to deliver this afternoon so I have a bit of free time.'

Lizzie was silent. It was frustrating enough not to be able to do this by herself. Feeling like Jack was picking up after her all the time was mortifying. Trying to distract herself, she looked around. There were staff members wearing Christmas accessories now. Reindeer antler headbands and flashing earrings. Two nurses were using a ladder to hang a string of bright silver baubles across the corridor. Jack had to manoeuvre the wheelchair carefully between them.

'It'll be the first time I'll be showing video footage of Misty's surgery,' he said into the silence between them. 'And yours.'

'Oh, help…Hollywood will be knocking on my door soon, then?'

His chuckle was delicious. 'I wouldn't hold your breath.'

'No.' She didn't even have a door anyone could knock on at the moment. The reminder of what lengths Jack had gone to for her made her take a deep breath. 'Seriously, Jack…I don't know how I can possibly thank you for everything.'

'There's no need,' Jack said quickly. 'No…honestly,' he added, having waited until two orderlies carrying overflowing boxes of Christmas decorations went past.

'New experiences are valuable and this is definitely a first for me.'

'You've pushed a wheelchair before,' she teased.

'That's not what I meant.' He stopped by the lift, angling the wheelchair so his face was visible. 'I was talking about getting rather more involved in the life of a patient I'm connected with.'

Was that how he saw her? And Misty? Simply two patients? The knot that was trying to form in Lizzie's gut made her side hurt.

'It's a bit of a no-no, isn't it? Getting involved with patients?'

Jack looked away. 'Officially, Misty isn't my patient. She's a starring model for my video documentary. And you're certainly not my patient. You're my...ah...'

'House guest?' Lizzie suggested wryly.

'No.' The head shake was decisive. 'You'd only be my house guest if I was living there as well.' He shrugged. 'It's an empty house. You needed a place to stay. End of story.'

Jack pushed the button to summon the lift, making it a punctuation mark. Someone had stencilled snowflakes onto the stainless-steel doors with spray-on snow.

It wasn't the whole story, though, was it?

With the kind of wealth that made hiring a car and chauffeur merely the inconvenience of making a phone call, Jack could probably have put them all up in a hotel to do his good deed. Why take them back to his own house?

'It's a very beautiful place to stay,' she said quietly. 'When I saw it in the daylight this morning, I couldn't believe the gardens. You've got a lake!'

'More a big pond,' he corrected.

'It's frozen over. You could probably skate on it.'

'I wouldn't advise trying. It used to be quite deep in the middle and the ice won't be that thick.'

Lizzie was smiling as the lift arrived. 'Don't worry. I'll make sure Holly doesn't go near it and I'm probably not up to skating just yet.'

She waited until the doors had shut before voicing a new fear.

'You don't think Dave Kingsley would really try and make me stay in hospital tonight, do you?'

'I think if you have a good rest for the afternoon, it might not come to anything. But if Dave still thinks it's a good idea, you'd be well advised to follow orders.'

'But—'

'It wouldn't be a problem. Kerry's taking the best care of Holly and I'll get my housekeeper to make sure they have everything they need for a day or two.'

'It's too much to ask,' Lizzie said firmly, shaking her head.

'You're not asking. I'm offering. And it's nothing… really. Consider it a Christmas gift.' She could hear the smile in his voice and had to look up to see it. 'I'm making up for being somewhat lax in my nelf duties lately.'

Oh…dear Lord…that *smile*.

He's just being kind, she told herself very firmly.

Because of Christmas.

Because he'd become interested in Misty's case and she had a twin sister, maybe. Funny how people were captured so easily by the twin thing. They found it intriguing and then, when they got to know her girls, they were captured even more. Of course they were. They were amazing children and she owed it to them to accept this kindness she was being offered on their behalf.

It was just for a little while. A gift because it was Christmas.

A gift she would feel thankful for and be able to remember for the rest of her life. A gift that would give her a connection to Jack Rousseau, maybe also for the rest of her life. Having that length of time to consider was good. It meant that when she felt better, she would be able to think of some way to repay him.

Maggie was just awake but still very sleepy.

'I'm still in the land of the living,' she murmured. 'And you're here, Lizzie...and Jack. How *very* nice.'

Jack stayed at the end of the bed, reading the medical chart, while Lizzie held her mother's hand.

'You're doing well, Mrs Donaldson. You came through with flying colours by the look of this.'

'Mum's as tough as they come.' Lizzie voice wobbled but she was smiling.

'Look who's talking,' Maggie mumbled. 'You have the lion's share of courage, love. And a heart as big as Texas.'

She did. Mother and daughter were smiling at each other so they couldn't see the way Jack let his gaze rest on Lizzie.

She was special, all right.

Amazing...

It was disconcertingly difficult to stop looking at her. And it was impossible to ignore that curl in his gut that only the most desirable of women could account for.

He went to find a staff member in the recovery room to talk to, then came back.

'You can stay for ten minutes,' he told Lizzie. 'I've found a nurse who's going to make sure you get delivered for your check-up downstairs. I'll give Dave a call and let him know when to expect you. I'd better get myself over to Hammersmith.'

It was a relief to step back into normality. To give himself time to sort his slide presentation and negotiate city traffic to get to an important engagement on time. This was what his life was all about. Delivering his skills to the expected level of competence. Professional interactions and enough pressure on both his skills and available time to make anything outside work hours almost irrelevant.

Taking even moments of time to be aware of fuzzy, emotional things like family bonds or the pleasure of a dog's company was an aberration. One that, disturbingly, seemed to be happening with increasing regularity. Throw in even the stirrings of physical desire and the combination was becoming downright dangerous.

Delivering this lecture to a packed auditorium in one of London's most prestigious hospitals was a very good thing. A dose of welcome reality.

The lecture was extremely well-received and led to an interesting question and answer session at the end about the advantages and disadvantages of peritoneal versus haemodialysis for young children.

'Is peritoneal still the preferred treatment for children?' someone queried.

'Yes, it is,' Jack responded. 'It can be done at home during the day or with the aid of a cycler machine at night. It causes less disruption to a daily routine and makes attendance at school much easier.'

'Why do haemodialysis at all, then?'

'The disadvantage of peritoneal dialysis is the heavy responsibility that is put on the carer, usually a parent. Stress levels can be elevated, which can have a detrimental effect on family dynamics.'

Jack was astonished at how easily the picture of a family coping with a child in end-stage renal failure came to his mind. In front of hundreds of eager students and respectful colleagues, all he could think of for several heartbeats was Lizzie and her twin daughters.

'And family,' he added slowly, 'to any child, is the whole world. To a sick child, it's something that has to be part of any holistic care.'

When he felt his mobile phone vibrating in his pocket at that point, his first thought was also Lizzie and the thought that something might have happened to her was chilling.

It was far more likely that Dave was calling him about one of his more complicated cases, but a quick glance at the caller ID showed him that the call was coming from his country house. No way could he ignore it and he'd already gone over the allocated lecture time. He excused himself from the lecture theatre and called back.

'I'm so sorry to bother you, Jack, but you said to call if I was worried about anything…'

'Kerry?' She sounded breathless. 'What's wrong?'

'Um…nothing *bad*, exactly…'

Jack thought of the iced-over pond he'd been talking to Lizzie about and felt another chill run down his spine. 'Is Holly all right?'

'She's great. We've been making gingerbread men and…'

He heard the catch in her voice. And the unnerving silence that followed.

'Kerry?'

'Phew…I think it's stopped.'

'What's stopped?'

'The contraction.'

Oh…*no*… Jack squeezed his eyes shut as he took in a very deep breath. He rubbed his forehead with his knuckles for good measure.

'How often are you getting contractions, Kerry?'

'Um…it was about five minutes between the last two.'

'OK. Listen to me.' Jack pulled in another breath. 'I'm going to call an ambulance. Lock Dougal in the house when they get there and you'll need to take Holly with you. I'll meet you at the hospital. They'll probably take you to St Bethel's Hospital, which is a lot closer than Westbridge. I'll meet you there. Ask the paramedics to call me if they take you anywhere else. Got it?'

'Got it…and…Jack?'

'Yes?' He really didn't want to be told how nice he was.

'Sorry.'

'Don't be. Can't be helped.' But Jack found himself staring at his phone as he snapped it shut.

This was turning into some kind of nightmare and he was trapped in it.

After directing an ambulance to the young woman in labour, he put in a call to Dave Kingsley.

'Lizzie's fine. All she needed was a few hours' sleep. I've told her she's fine to go home but they've put her mother into the coronary care unit for a few hours. She had a bit of an arrhythmia when they were about to transfer her from Recovery to the ward and they want to monitor her cardiac activity carefully for a while. Lizzie's decided to stay with her but has promised to try and get some more sleep. She said she had someone she trusted completely to look after Holly.'

Did she need the extra worry of knowing that the person she trusted to care for her daughter was about to be collected by an ambulance and that she would have Holly in tow as she travelled to a strange hospital to give birth?

No, of course she didn't. She certainly wouldn't get any rest if she knew.

'Tell her everything else is completely under control,' he told Dave. 'She doesn't need to worry.'

He could do that much for her. Just for tonight and that would be it. His level of involvement here was becoming absurd.

Kerry was in a cubicle in the A and E department of St Bethel's, a small hospital on the outskirts of London.

'Wouldn't you know it?' she groaned. 'The contractions stopped the minute I got in here.'

'We're going to admit her overnight just to keep an eye on her,' the consultant told Jack.

'No!' Kerry looked as alarmed as Jack was feeling. 'I have to go home.'

'Those contractions could start again.' The consultant was scanning notes a registrar had already made. 'And from the looks of this, your antenatal care has been a bit...patchy. It would be prudent to have a good check-up.'

'Indeed it would.' Jack knew his voice sounded hollow. He tried to smile. 'I'm no obstetrician. You don't want me having to try and remember med school training at 3:00 a.m.'

The consultant was looking curious. 'You're a doctor?'

'Transplant specialist. Jack Rousseau.'

'I've heard the name.' They shook hands and the emergency department consultant raised an eyebrow. 'And you and Kerry are...ah...'

'No.' Kerry spoke up swiftly. 'Jack's being kind enough to let us stay in his house, that's all. We had an explosion in our apartment block last night.'

'Oh?' The consultant blinked. 'And the little girl who came in with you?'

'She's my neighbour's granddaughter. I'm friends with her mum. So's Jack.'

It was getting too confusing for the St Bethel's doctor, who shook his head in bemusement. Jack was very tempted to mirror the action. Instead, he turned to Kerry.

'Where *is* Holly?'

'A nurse said she was taking her to the relatives' room.'

'I'll take her home. My housekeeper, Mrs Benny, will look after her. You need to do what the doctors here advise.'

He didn't give Kerry any time to argue. He got directions to the relatives' room but paused on the way to ring his housekeeper.

'I'll be bringing a child home for the night,' he informed her. 'I'd like you to take care of her.'

The voice on the other end of the line was tight. 'You can manage without me, you said. As far as I'm concerned, Dr Rousseau, my employment with you has been terminated.'

Mrs Benny hung up on him.

Jack would have laughed aloud at this new twist in his personal nightmare but he had turned his head for some reason and now he could see into the relatives' room he'd been heading towards.

Whatever staff member had taken Holly there hadn't stayed with her. The small girl was sitting alone in an empty room.

Just sitting, with her hands clasped in her lap and an expression on her face that made Jack's throat tighten so much it was too hard to take a breath.

He *knew* that look.

This was why he avoided children. Why he'd put off the thought of ever getting involved enough to consider getting married or having a family of his own. It wasn't that children, or women for that matter, were so inclined to cry.

It was that *neediness*.

His memory was so accurate he could feel, deep inside himself, what it was like to be a child like that. So vulnerable and desperate. Or rather he knew what it felt to be like that and to not receive what was so desperately needed.

The misery of wanting something that wasn't there.

The responsibility of being the one expected to provide it. *That* was what was terrifying about marriage and children.

How could he ever give something that he'd never been given himself? He didn't know how.

Jack still hadn't moved. Not one step closer to Holly.

He didn't have to give this little girl what she needed most, though, did he?

She had it in spades. She had the most amazing mother. A grandmother. A sister. A neighbour who was more like a family member. She even had a dog that loved her.

A home she would be able to return to soon enough. People to love and be loved by.

This space of time was an anomaly. A crevasse in a normally emotionally secure life. He'd seen what the connection was like in this little family, that day when they'd been clustered around Misty's bed. Maybe fate had decreed that he would be in the right place at the right time, to make a bridge across that crevasse for Holly.

Just for now.

For Christmas?

She had begged Santa for a daddy for Christmas, hadn't she?

Not for ever.

Just for Christmas.

That was only a matter of days away and by the time Christmas was over, everything would be sorted. Lizzie would be well on the road to complete recovery. Maggie would be close to being back on her feet. Their home would be safe.

A bridge. That was all he needed to be.

A temporary daddy?

As if she'd finally sensed his presence in the corridor, Holly looked up. The fear and loneliness and need was still etched on her face but there was something different in the way she looked now. Or the way she was sitting, maybe.

Jack could actually feel the ripple of hope coming out to wash over *him*.

He held out his hand. 'Come on, Holly. It's time to go home.'

CHAPTER EIGHT

THERE was a supermarket on the route from St Bethel's to Jack's house.

'Dog food,' Jack muttered to himself. 'And milk.' He glanced over his shoulder. 'What do you want for your dinner, Holly?'

How bizarre was this? He'd never had to think about feeding a dog, let alone cooking for a child. Up till now, the most difficult meal decisions he'd ever had to make had been which gourmet restaurant to take someone like Danielle to and whether he could secure the most impressive table.

It seemed like a different life now. Right now, it should seem as alluring as, say, a tropical island holiday. Very odd that it seemed surreal and…meaningless.

'Sketti,' Holly said decisively.

'Sketti?' Jack's English was close to perfect after the years of boarding and then medical school but this was a new word for him. 'What's that?' Some kind of fish, maybe?

'*You* know.' Holly's tone was very patient. 'It goes on toast. Me and Misty call it worms sometimes but only when Mummy can't hear us.'

'Oh…' Comprehension came with a clunk. *'Spaghetti.'*

'Mmm. Sketti.'

'And what does Dougal eat?'

'Crunchy brown things. They don't taste very nice. He likes sketti better.'

Jack found an empty slot in the supermarket car park. He was still shaking his head as he went round to open the back door. 'How do you know that Dougal's food doesn't taste very nice? Do *you* eat dog food, too?'

Holly's eyes went very wide. She pressed her lips together firmly.

'Never mind.' Jack led the way into the supermarket. He was taken by surprise when Holly's hand slipped into his but maybe it was a good idea to keep a hold of it. He wouldn't want to lose her in the crowd.

Holly wanted to sit in the trolley. 'Cos my legs are sleepy,' she said.

She sat at the far end, with her knees drawn up to make room for the grocery items, including several cans of spaghetti and a loaf of bread. Halfway down the dairy aisle on their way to find butter, Jack suddenly realised he was actually enjoying himself. This was definitely a new experience. He'd never pushed a supermarket trolley before, let alone one that had a very cute, small girl directing proceedings. She was pointing imperiously now.

'*That* butter. Kerry says it's the bestest.'

New Zealand butter. That figured. Jack made a mental note to call St Bethel's later and check up on how Kerry was doing. He'd have to contact Lizzie somehow, too, but that was a little more problematic. With a sigh,

Jack pushed the issue aside and went in search of the dog food aisle.

The supermarket was busy and the shoppers were predominantly women. By the time they got to the checkout, Jack was aware of how many looks he was getting, along with some rather impressed-looking smiles. The girl at the till provided a clue to the puzzle.

'Ooh, aren't you lucky,' she said to Holly. 'You get to go shopping with your *daddy*.'

Jack's heart skipped a beat. Any second now and Holly would say that he wasn't her daddy. He'd get a rather different kind of look then and goodness knows what kind of trouble he might find himself in.

The thought was alarming to say the least. The alarm almost, but not quite, obliterated that odd buzz he'd got from someone assuming he was Holly's father.

To his surprise, Holly said nothing at all. She gave Jack the oddest look and then simply smiled, picking up a can of spaghetti to put onto the conveyor belt.

'Quiet little thing, aren't you?' The checkout girl winked at Jack. 'My favourite kind of kid.'

Jack smiled at her. 'Mine, too.'

Dougal was overjoyed to have company and seemed thrilled by Jack's choice of kibbled dog food. He saw Holly eyeing the dog's enthusiasm for the new food.

'No,' he said, sternly. 'Don't even think about it. We've got sketti, remember?'

At least toasting and buttering bread and heating canned spaghetti were well within Jack's culinary skill level. Strangely, it didn't even taste that bad.

Holly finally pushed her plate away 'I'm as full as a bull,' she announced.

Her face was covered with tomato sauce.

'You need a wash,' Jack told her. A worrying thought occurred to him. 'Are you old enough to have a bath by yourself?'

Holly nodded. 'I'm *six*.' She screwed her face into deeply thoughtful lines. 'The taps are hard, though. I've just got little fingers.'

'I'll run it for you.'

He stayed within shouting distance, too, sitting on the top stair with Dougal beside him while Holly was in the bath. He'd go in, he decided, if the singing and splashing sounds diminished into silence.

It was a good time to ring St Bethel's and he learned that Kerry was sound asleep. The contractions, probably Braxton Hicks', had stopped completely and she'd be able to go home in the morning.

The worry of what to say to Lizzie sorted itself with remarkable ease when *his* phone rang.

'Oh…Jack…I was expecting it to be Kerry.'

'She's having a bit of a rest.'

'Is she all right?'

'Yes.' He was telling the truth. Some of it, anyway. 'She had a few Braxon Hicks' contractions today but they've stopped now.'

'And Holly? Is she all right?'

From the corner of his eye, Jack could see a small, naked figure, trailing a towel by one corner and moving purposefully into the bedroom.

'She's getting her pyjamas on. Do you want to talk to her?'

'Please.'

Holly had her pyjamas on inside out. 'Mummy…we had *sketti* for tea.'

She listened for a while, nodding vigorously and then her face lit up with a joyous smile. 'I love you too, Mummy. Ni' night.'

The phone was handed back to Jack. 'How are *you*?' he asked.

'I'm fine. All I needed was a bit of sleep. And Mum's fine, too. They've shifted her back to the ward and she's actually been up on her feet just to see how she went. I could leave but it's getting late and it would nice to be able to check up on Mum *and* Misty first thing in the morning.'

'Of course it would.' Jack brushed aside the desire to send a car to collect her immediately to bring her back here. 'Try and get some sleep, won't you? I'll get Kerry to call you in the morning.'

'Thanks.'

Lizzie sounded tired, which was hardly surprising given such an emotional day. Was he wrong in not telling her about Kerry? Or that he was alone in the house with Holly, pretending to be her daddy?

Probably. But it had seemed the right thing to do.

So was making sure that Holly got into bed and snuggled up. The child's eyes were drooping enough to suggest that sleep was not far away.

She was an astonishing kid, Jack decided. She hadn't been any trouble at all, really. Except that, when he said good night and turned to leave, her little jaw wobbled ominously.

'It'll be all right,' Jack assured her. 'Kerry *and*

Mummy will most likely be home tomorrow to look after you. And it'll *be* tomorrow as soon as you've had a sleep.'

'But I can't go to sleep.'

'Why not?'

'Cos Mummy always gives me a love. And if she's not there, Nanna gives me a love. Or Kerry does. Sometimes Dougal does, too.'

Jack eyed the dog hopefully. Dougal stayed where he was at the end of the bed and thumped his tail.

Holly sniffed loudly.

'Um…' Surely Holly could sense how far out of his depth he was? Apparently not. Big blue eyes were fixed on him. 'I'm not sure I know about giving loves,' Jack muttered.

'It's easy.' Holly was out from under the covers like a shot. She stood on the bed and held her arms out. 'You just have to do this.'

He simply couldn't *not* do it. Jack opened his own arms and found himself hugging a small girl whose arms clung tightly around his neck.

She was so small. So fragile. He could feel her heart beating rapidly against his chest and hear her snuffling against his neck. He could smell soap and warmth and… something that reminded him of summer.

The neediness was certainly there but he seemed to be doing enough with nothing more than holding her. Or being there for her to hold. The fierce tension ebbed from the tight grip and Holly's sigh a short time later was contented. Jack bent down and the little girl obligingly slithered free and buried her face in the pillows.

By the time Jack pulled up the covers to keep her warm, she appeared to be soundly asleep.

The dog gave him an approving look and padded after Jack but they both stopped at the bedroom door and turned back for a final glance.

Jack could still feel those small arms around him and the incredible softness of the hair that had tickled his skin. He could see the stain of tomato sauce that hadn't quite been vanquished by the bath. Most of all, he could see the echo of this child's smile when her mother must have told her she was loved and hear the sound of that contented little sigh after his hug.

It was doing something very strange, deep inside his gut. He could feel an odd, almost melting sensation. A liquid feeling that puddled around something very solid that he recognised as a desire to protect this small person.

Bemused at the overpowering strength of this new sensation, Jack went slowly downstairs and from out of nowhere he remembered something else he'd heard Holly telling Father Christmas.

Mummy looks after everybody. Me and Misty and Nanna. But there's nobody to take care of Mummy, is there? I'm still too little.

She wanted to, though, didn't she? This child had the same kind of heart as her mother. As big as Texas.

Jack could feel that sensation tightening inside him. Squeezing his heart.

Holly deserved something special. For herself. Something she could remember for the rest of her life.

But what?

Jack thought about it as sipped his vintage bourbon.

He discussed it with Dougal when he took the dog out into the garden for a spell before closing up the house for the night.

And then it occurred to him. Christmas was important in this family for an extra reason. It was also the twins' birthday. What if—*this* year—it was really, really special? A combination Christmas birthday celebration that had everything two little girls could wish for?

A day that they would remember for ever.

So would he, because he would play at least a small part in it—*be* there—so that he could make their Christmas wish come true. And that really would be the end of it. He could cut short this consultancy stint by pleading pressure from his Paris base or something and then he would be gone. He could put this property on the market and never come back. It might take months to sell and Lizzie and her family could stay here until it did and that would give them plenty of time to get their own lives back in order.

The solution seemed neat. He could help, give them all something nice to remember and tuck it into the past and move on. The question now was how on earth could he make it happen? Research was called for and, at this time of night, the internet was the only place to start.

A Christmas tree shouldn't be a problem. His gardener, Jimmy, could no doubt source one out in the woods but this needed to make more of a statement than a small branch of a spruce tree. He'd seen thousands of those impressive kinds of trees very recently, though, hadn't he? The day he'd happened to eavesdrop on Holly talking to Father Christmas, in fact, which made it perfectly logical to go looking for an online branch of Bennett's department store.

The array of goods available was mind-boggling. The variety of the usual trappings of Christmas-like trees and decorations and even food for a special meal seemed limitless but Jack kept scrolling through page after page, searching for an X factor of some kind.

He needed something…

Ah…the word in the sidebar said it all.

Personal.

He clicked on the 'Personal Shopper' tab and eyed a screen full of photographs and profiles. These were people who were specialist shoppers who promised they could do whatever it took to make Christmas magic for that special someone. They could take care of any decorations and catering and personal gifts. All they needed was a link that would provide enough background information.

One of the photos caught Jack's eye. A young man by the name of Barnaby who stood out as being a bit different, with his flop of black hair covering one eye, a ring in the visible eyebrow and a distinctly mischievous smile. It made him think of Kerry and she would know far more than he did about the twins and other members of the Matthews family. He could engage the services of this Barnaby with some general information to grab his attention and then make Kerry the link to the family and the two of them could go to town. All he would have to do was to provide the details of his credit card and give them a very generous budget.

Perfect.

Jack clicked on Barnaby's profile and scrolled to

the box to tell him who he'd be shopping for. He wrote about twin six-year-old girls, one of whom was due home for both Christmas and her birthday following a kidney transplant. He added a bit about their mother who had donated a kidney and the grandmother who was in need of some special care herself. He even put in a bit about Dougal. Nobody could read this little story without being moved, he decided. Hopefully, it would present a challenge that a personal shopper could rise to with the utmost determination to shine.

The sense of satisfaction in putting his plan into action so effectively was only equalled by the astonishment of realising how much time he had spent on this. And if it was 2:00 a.m., why on earth was his phone ringing?

'Sorry to wake you, Jack.'

'I wasn't asleep, Dave. What's happening?'

'I've got a kidney on the way down from Edinburgh. It's a good match for our MVA guy you know about but, given the complications we've got with his other abdominal injuries, I could really use your input on this surgery. Any chance you could get here in an hour or so?'

'Of course.' The response was automatic. It wasn't until Jack ended the call and went to pick up his car keys that he realised what he'd done.

He had a child asleep upstairs.

A child he was responsible for.

A groan escaped his lips. Had he really thought he could play at being a temporary daddy? Just for Christmas? Good grief…he couldn't even manage it for a single night.

He couldn't leave her.

But he couldn't not respond to the call. This was what he did. Who he *was*.

He could sort this, he decided, his mind working at the speed of light. If he took Holly in to the hospital with him, there would be a staff member who could care for her. An on-call room, probably, where she could be tucked up and continue sleeping with minimal disruption. It was far from ideal but it was, at least, a solution to the awful conflict he was still grappling with as he moved swiftly up the stairs. When he got to Holly's room, he stood for a moment, looking down at the perfect picture of a peacefully sleeping child.

This was *exactly* why it had been so unwise to allow himself any kind of involvement with Holly and her family. But he hadn't listened to the warning bells, had he? He'd allowed himself to get sucked in. Right from the moment his attention had been caught by the conversation Holly had been having with Father Christmas. Bit by bit, despite resisting, he'd been drawn closer and now here he was, facing the wake-up call.

It wasn't pleasant. His career meant that other people ended up being neglected and hurt. It had been bad enough to fail an adult partner who'd chosen to be with him knowing how he felt about his career but this time, he was failing an innocent child and it was, quite simply, unacceptable.

Holly whimpered but didn't wake up completely as he picked her up and wrapped her in the quilt.

'It's all right,' he murmured, 'We just need to go for a ride in the car.'

He carried the warm, sleepy bundle that was Holly

downstairs and out into an icy night. She made another, distressed sound as he tucked her into the car seat and fastened the safety belt.

He leaned closer. *'Je suis vraiment désolé, ma chérie,'* he whispered. 'This won't happen again, I promise.'

CHAPTER NINE

'I DON'T *believe* this.'

Lizzie stared at Kerry in horror as she sucked in a new breath. '*Any* of it. He didn't even tell me you were in hospital, let alone…'

Her voice trailed off. The enormity of what had happened overnight, which she had known nothing about, was too much.

'He was being nice,' Kerry assured her. 'And it all worked out fine, didn't it? He sent the car to get me this morning and we collected Holly and went back home to get clothes and the dolls and stuff. Hey…you should have seen old Stubby's face when we turned up with a *chauffeur.*'

Lizzie didn't care how gobsmacked Mr Stubbs had been. Or that Holly was triumphantly carrying the bag of well-worn dolls and their paraphernalia that Misty was desperate to play with now that she was feeling so much better.

'He had no right taking over like that. I didn't have to stay here. I certainly wouldn't have if I'd known where you were. Or that Jack was looking after Holly by himself. Heavens…*Mum* would have had a fit if she'd known about that.'

'We had sketti for tea,' Holly piped up, sending a worried frown in her mother's direction.

'Lucky you.' Kerry grinned. She sent Lizzie a glance that suggested she might want to tone things down in front of Holly. 'It's all fine now,' she said calmly. 'I was in the place I needed to be and so were you. Jack didn't want to worry you any more, that's all. It's not that big a deal. He didn't want you *or* your mum having any kind of fit. How's Maggie doing, anyway?'

'She's great. Determined to finish making those felt stockings for the girls before she gets home.' Lizzie managed a tight smile for Holly's benefit but she could feel the knot of tension inside her continuing to expand.

What was Jack Rousseau's deal?

Being interested in the lives of particular patients was one thing. Being so kind to people in trouble at Christmastime was another. Slightly harder to accept but understandable. That he thought he could assume control of her family affairs without even consulting her was definitely a step too far. It wasn't acceptable at all.

'We'll go and visit Misty,' she announced. 'And Nanna. And then we're going to go and collect Dougal and go home.'

Holly's frown was puzzled now. 'But Dougal *is* at home.'

'He's at Jack's home.' Lizzie knew she sounded grim but she couldn't help it. The time had come to pull the plug on this fantasy they had all been caught up in. 'We have to go back to our own home.'

She shouldn't have let Jack become involved at all. She could have prevented it. Right back at the start when she'd had the chance to deny his involvement with Misty and herself in making that documentary video.

Nelf law had been her undoing. Not to mention that ill-advised fantasy about the man with the sexy accent and the dark, chocolate eyes. God help her, but she only had to see those eyes or that smile of his to get drawn back to that fantasy every time.

This was her doing, all of it. And it had led to her child being dragged from her bed in the middle of the night because the man looking after her had had bigger responsibilities.

Well, she didn't have. From now on, it was the welfare of her family that would take precedence and any personal inclination to spend more time in Jack's presence would have to be ruthlessly crushed.

It was probably just as well that her path didn't cross that of Jack's during the hours they were at the hospital that day. Misty and Holly had a happy time playing dollies and some of her anger faded as she and Kerry watched them and simply enjoyed the progress Misty was clearly making in getting back to being a normal, healthy little girl.

Time with her mother was just as rewarding. A volunteer choir was doing the rounds, singing traditional Christmas songs and carols and handing out warm mince pies. A physiotherapist was also there, giving Maggie her first lesson in using elbow crutches.

'I'll be back tomorrow and we'll get you taking a step or two,' she said to Maggie. 'You'll be moving properly within a day or two and when you can manage stairs, you'll be allowed to go home.'

She wouldn't be able to manage ten flights of stairs, Lizzie thought with dismay. She would have to keep her fingers firmly crossed that the lifts in the tenement block didn't have one of their all–too-regular periods of being out of action. In the new year, she vowed, she would start looking for somewhere else for them all to live. Somehow, she would make it happen.

By mid-afternoon, they were ready to go and collect Dougal and Lizzie was faced with a new dilemma. The car and chauffeur would be waiting nearby but maybe this was the moment to assert her independence and call a taxi. To hire a taxi to go all the way out to Jack's country house and then take them back again would be prohibitively expensive, however, and she wasn't even sure she had the funds available on her card.

It was Jack's fault that they were so far out of the city, though, wasn't it?

Or was it all her fault for allowing their rescue the other night instead of joining her neighbours at what-ever shelter had been provided?

A compromise was the best option, she decided. She would use the car to get out there and then tell the driver his services would no longer be needed. They would get a taxi home.

An hour or so later, the wheels of the luxury car crunched over the thin layer of snow on the pebbled driveway of the country estate. The vehicle couldn't get close to the front steps, however, because an enormous truck was parked there.

A Bennett's truck.

Lounging near the rear of the truck was a young man with floppy, black hair and a gold ring glinting in his eyebrow.

Kerry was as transfixed by the apparition as Lizzie was but clearly for a very different reason.

'Who *is* that?' she breathed. 'Oh, my God…he's…*gorgeous*.'

'What's in the truck?' Holly sounded just as excited as Kerry.

'Why is it here?' Lizzie muttered, perplexed. 'What on earth is going on here?'

Despite her advanced state of pregnancy, Kerry was first out of the car. Holly bounced after her. By the time Lizzie joined them, Kerry and the young man were busy grinning at each other.

'This is Barnaby,' Kerry informed her.

'I think you might have the wrong address,' Lizzie told him.

'Don't think so.' Barnaby flicked his glossy hair so that, briefly, both his eyes were visible. 'You're Lizzie Matthews, aren't you?'

'Yes.'

Barnaby gaze slid away again instantly. 'And you're Kerry, aren't you?'

'Oh, my God…you're psychic, aren't you?'

They grinned at each other again.

'I'm Holly,' Holly said, standing on tiptoe and tugging at Barnaby's sleeve.

'I know that, princess.' He tore his gaze away from Kerry and ruffled Holly's curls. 'And you have a twin sister called Misty who's in hospital and a grandma who's in hospital too.'

Lizzie's jaw dropped. 'How do you know that?'

She knew, though, didn't she? Not only was Jack taking over control in her life, he was broadcasting personal information to all and sundry.

Barnaby had the cheek to wink at her. 'Cos I'm psychic?'

Holly tugged at his sleeve again. 'Why are *you* sick?'

But Barnaby just grinned. He held out his arms like a conjuror about to dazzle them all with a magic trick. 'I'm your personal shopper,' he told them.

Lizzie's breath left her in an incredulous huff. Barnaby's grin faded. 'Maybe I should explain?'

'I think you'd better.' Lizzie folded her arms tightly in front of her as though she needed to give herself a hug. 'Kerry? Do you think you and Holly could go and let Dougal out or something?'

'Sure…' Kerry cast a final glance in Barnaby's direction. 'I guess. Come on, Prickles.'

Lizzie glared at Barnaby as soon as the others were out of earshot but before he could even open his mouth to start talking, another vehicle came racing down the driveway. She could see Jack staring at the Bennett's truck as he came to halt but it was Lizzie who had his full attention when he came to join them.

'I need to explain,' he said.

Dougal came barrelling out of the house at full speed and went straight to Jack, planting already grubby paws on his immaculate merino coat.

'Down,' Jack commanded, moving away. He turned towards the open area of the garden and issued another command. 'Come with me.'

Lizzie thought he was talking to the dog but then he touched her arm. 'Please?' he added.

Without thinking, she obeyed the direction.

'Um…I'll go and have a chat with Kerry, shall I?' Barnaby called after them.

'Good idea,' Jack said, without turning back.

They walked to the edge of the lawn and watched Dougal ploughing furrows and then rolling in the snow, stopping only to lift his leg on a tree here and there. It was cold but Lizzie just rubbed at her arms. She had things to say to Jack that would be better said in privacy. Angry things about assuming control and putting her child at risk.

But Jack was shedding his coat. He draped it over Lizzie's shoulders.

'This is all my fault,' he said. 'I'm so sorry, Lizzie.'

The apology was so unexpected, Lizzie searched his face. 'What for?'

'I shouldn't have brought Holly here last night. I wasn't on call but, in my line of work, I'm never completely *off* call. I didn't think.'

'No. You didn't.' Lizzie was amazed to hear sadness rather than anger in her own voice.

Jack pushed his fingers through his hair. He was standing in his shirtsleeves but he didn't seem to be cold yet. Lizzie wasn't cold at all. She was wrapped in warmth that smelt like Jack and it was…delicious.

They walked a little further, through the archway of a beautifully clipped, round yew hedge that sheltered a water feature.

'I don't know quite how it happened,' Jack said. 'It certainly wasn't intentional. That's why I'm single, you know. Why I'll always be single, because I would never set out to let anybody down like that.'

Suddenly, berating Jack for what had happened seemed wrong.

Part of her brain was trying to replay his words. Trying to hammer home the message that Jack was choosing to be single. That he intended to remain single. Unattached. Unencumbered.

'There was no harm done,' Lizzie said slowly. 'And I do understand that you were only trying to help.'

'I shouldn't have. I'm not in a position to give that kind of help. I shouldn't have tried.'

Dougal did a circuit of the round garden room and then vanished again, barking to share his joy at being free to run.

Lizzie wanted to change the subject. Or not. Why was Jack beating himself up so much over this? OK, he'd taken a sleeping child from her bed in the middle of the night but he hadn't abandoned her, had he? And he hadn't told her about any of it because he'd known she'd had enough on her plate last night, worrying about her mother.

'You've been incredibly helpful,' she told him now. 'I can never thank you enough. But what I don't understand is...'

He was watching her face carefully. Listening to every word she said. Lizzie could feel the pull between them. Something that was powerful and real but they were both ignoring it. Why?

That was what she didn't understand. Why it was there. What it really was and whether it meant anything like what it felt like it *could* mean.

Was it simply humanitarian interest on Jack's part? A series of coincidences that was pulling them closer? Was it gratitude on her part? Loneliness maybe and feeling more vulnerable because she wasn't a hundred per cent healthy yet? All this with a bit of physical attraction thrown in?

No.

Lizzie's gaze hadn't left Jack's face. She knew every line of it now, she realised. The crinkles at the corners of his eyes, the aristocratic shape of his nose, the furrows that defined the edges of his cheeks and led to lips that were capable of giving the most beautiful smiles on earth.

He might not want it—in fact, he obviously didn't, having made his declaration that he would be single for ever—and she might not want to give it, having vowed to nurture her independence—but this man had Lizzie's heart.

For better or worse, she *loved* him.

Oh...God. He was still waiting for her to finish her sentence. Watching her face as if he could read her thoughts.

'The truck,' she croaked, a trifle desperately. 'I don't understand what the truck is doing here.'

'Ah...' Jack's eyes told her that he knew that wasn't what she'd been thinking about at all. His tone suggested relief that this was something he could deal with. 'It's here because of...Holly.'

'Holly?'

'Mmm.' Jack's gaze still hadn't left hers. There was an unspoken message going on but Lizzie couldn't figure out what it was. Neither could she look away. She watched the way the corners of Jack's mouth tilted up a little. A close enough reminder of one of his smiles to make her aware of a melting sensation in her chest.

'It's to do with what I heard Holly asking Father Christmas for that day.'

Lizzie's inward breath was almost a gasp. Was he going to tell her? Was he going to make her daughters' wish come true?

'It's in the truck? What they wished for?'

'Not…exactly.'

It was childish, but Lizzie was tempted to stamp her foot.

'Tell me…*please*, Jack. This is really important. If there's something they really want for Christmas and I can provide it for them, I really want to be able to do that. I'll do anything to make a wish come true for them at the moment.'

'Anything?'

There was a low note in Jack's voice. Perhaps amusement was part of it but it came across as a rumble that had purely sexual connotations. Lizzie could feel a wash of heat rising from her belly towards her face and, for a heartbeat, the world seemed to hold its breath.

Rather like the way Jack was holding Lizzie's gaze.

What would he want from her if she said yes?

Perhaps a more relevant question would be what *wasn't* she prepared to give him?

Dear Lord… Lizzie had to close her eyes and remind herself to breathe. And then she had to look away because it was simply too dangerous to let that astonishingly intimate gaze continue for even a moment longer.

Jack cleared his throat but his voice still sounded curiously hoarse.

'I can't tell you,' he said apologetically.

Lizzie gave a resigned huff. 'Nelf law again?'

'I'm afraid so.'

She risked a quick glance. He was still looking down at her. He still had a hint of a smile playing with his lips.

'But I can provide it,' he added.

'You mean...*buy* it?' Perhaps he had already and whatever it was was stowed in the Bennett's truck. 'Jack, I can't let you—'

His head shake was subtle but enough to stop her talking. 'It's a bit more complicated than that. It's all about a...setting as much as anything else.'

'What kind of setting?'

'A Christmas kind. A tree with decorations. Presents. Food and people. Particular people.'

'Like who?' Lizzie could see that Jack was finally feeling the cold. He was rubbing his hands together and she could see goose-bumps where the cuffs of his shirt ended.

'You, of course. And your mother. Kerry, too. Me, even.' The last words were added casually but to Lizzie they resonated with a particular significance.

Had Holly wished for a special Christmas Day? The kind that was idealised in children's stories? With a snow-covered garden and a big house full of warmth and light and the joys of an extended family?

Was it part of the twins' wish that Jack be included?

No. How could it have been when the wish had been made before they'd even known he existed?

As unlikely as it might seem, it was a possibility that it was Jack's wish to be a part of it.

He was single. Did he even have a family of his own to be with?

He might be dedicated to his high-profile career to the degree of allowing nothing personal to compromise that dedication, but there had to be times when he felt like he was missing out.

When he felt lonely, even.

Lizzie had the odd sensation that something was breaking inside her. A tiny piece of her heart, maybe.

'Oh…Jack,' she whispered. 'Is that what the truck is all about? Are you trying to make Christmas for us all?'

He didn't say anything. He just stood there, looking down at Lizzie with an appeal in his eyes that she couldn't possibly resist.

All her earlier resolve melted into oblivion. How on earth could she pack up and take Holly and Dougal and Kerry back to their tenement housing? It wasn't that it would ruin their own Christmas. She could manage to make a special day for them all but, if she did that, she would be taking away the opportunity Jack had to have a real, family kind of Christmas.

With songs and laughter and the kind of magic that only small children could bring to a family celebration. If she left, she would be leaving Jack alone in an empty house. She could imagine him coming out into this garden, in the snow, alone and…cold.

Impetuously, Lizzie opened her arms and slipped them around Jack to hug him. To offer him some warmth. To accept this incredibly generous offer. She couldn't reject it because, if she did, she would be rejecting *him*. Most of all, she wanted the hug to say thank you. To say that she understood.

For a moment, Lizzie could feel his surprise at her gesture but then his body softened a little and his arms came around her. He pulled the coat back over her shoulders to keep her warm but then they stayed around her. Pulling her closer, even.

Had she really thought he looked cold? His body was so warm. Alive. She could feel the thump of his heart and the strength of his chest as it rose and fell with each breath.

The pull that had been there between them all along was a liquid thing now and Lizzie was drowning in it. She looked up, intending to smile before pushing herself away so that she could breathe again.

But Jack's arms still held her and when she raised her face, it was to find him still looking down at her, with something like amazement in his eyes. Was he feeling the same, overwhelming pull?

Lizzie couldn't be sure who moved first. Did she stand on tiptoe, like Holly did when she really wanted to be noticed? Or did Jack dip his head and she had been powerless to resist meeting him halfway?

The moment their lips touched, it ceased to matter.

The world didn't just hold its breath this time.

It stopped turning.

CHAPTER TEN

JACK ROUSSEAU had kissed many women in his life.

He'd always been attracted to those he chose to kiss. He had been in love with the woman he'd chosen as his wife so many years ago.

So many women. So many kisses.

But not one of those kisses had been remotely like this one.

He wasn't sure how it had happened. He'd only intended to talk to Lizzie. To explain the emergency situation that had led to him dragging poor Holly from her bed last night and to apologise for it. He'd also needed to explain the presence of that Bennett's truck, which had meant telling her about his late-night internet activity and his desire to make Christmas special, for Holly in particular.

But something had happened. Some kind of connection had occurred when that joke about nelf law had been resurrected. As if it was a key of some kind that had taken them back to their first conversation, when Lizzie had chosen to honour him with her trust.

He had seen her passion for her children in the determination to discover their Christmas wish and make it come true. And then he'd seen something he remembered from that scene when he'd been with the whole family just after Misty's surgery. It was that same kind of warmth in Lizzie's eyes that drew him in and made him feel a part of something. Made him feel…wanted.

To have her looking at him like that and then feel her arms around his body. To have her face tilted up, so close to his own, and see those soft, inviting lips parted just a little.

Well…what was a man to do? Resisting the urge to touch those lips with his own was inconceivable.

Just a touch. A mere brush.

But something else had happened then, hadn't it? Like the way he'd felt them connect with that eye contact minutes ago. Except that where the earlier connection had been like the glow of comforting embers, this one that came with the touch of their lips was a blazing inferno.

Mon Dieu.

He'd never felt such desire that wrangled with such tenderness. He wanted to make love to this woman, of course, but it was more than that. He wanted to worship every inch of her body. With his hands, his lips… his heart…

The sound of a dog barking was distant.

An irate voice with a heavy Scottish accent was not.

'Ye blithering mongrel. Away wi' you.'

Jack let go of Lizzie and stepped back just in time.

'Jack! What in heaven's name are you doing out here in the snow and ice, lad?'

'Jimmy.' He had to smile at a man who never seemed to change, except that he had become far less frightening than he'd seemed when Jack had been a child. 'How are you?'

But Jimmy was scowling at Lizzie, who was looking completely stunned. Her lips were pink and plump from his attention and they were still parted, but she wasn't looking at Jack. She was staring at the giant of a man who'd come through the hedge archway.

'This is Jimmy,' Jack explained. 'My groundsman.'

'I just came to check on the boiler and see if any snow needed shovelling,' Jimmy growled. 'And I find there's a blithering great lorry parked in the way. And this...*dog*.' He glared at Dougal who was sitting, gazing adoringly up at him, his tail sweeping arcs of snow from the neatly mown grass.

'The *truck*,' Lizzie murmured, as though she'd completely forgotten what they'd been talking about prior to that kiss.

She wasn't the only one. With a sigh, Jack realised he had rather a lot to sort out.

'I'll get it sorted,' he told Jimmy. 'It's getting a bit dark to shovel snow anyway, isn't it? Perhaps you could leave it until tomorrow?'

'Aye...' Jimmy's bushy black eyebrows were lowered as he stared at Lizzie again. 'This is *your* dog?'

'Um...yes...'

'He was digging a hole in the rose garden.'

'Oh...I'm sorry. I'll keep a better eye on him.'

'Lizzie's staying here at the moment, Jimmy,' Jack said. 'With her family.'

The eyebrows rose sharply and Jimmy seemed lost for words. Then he gave Lizzie another glower. Finally his mouth curved in a reluctant half-smile.

'Aye…well…I'll make sure I keep on top of the snow, then.'

With that, he turned and stomped away, leaving Dougal sitting remarkably still and straight, gazing longingly after the departing figure. Jack was standing close enough to Lizzie to feel her shiver and his fingers were beginning to tingle painfully with the cold.

'We'd better go inside,' he said.

'Mmm.' Lizzie gave her head a tiny shake. Returning to reality, perhaps? 'I think we should.'

It was utterly confusing.

Dougal followed them into the house and was leaving a trail of muddy pawprints on the flagged floor of the kitchen. Holly was bouncing up and down and trying to tell her something. Barnaby and Kerry were sitting at the kitchen table with Bennett's catalogues spread out in front of them and they both seemed to be laughing and talking at the same time.

Lizzie couldn't make head or tail of any of it.

All she could think about was that kiss.

The *heat* of it.

The sheer desire that had curled her toes and made her forget about…well, everything.

All the stress that had been steadily accumulating over the last months and weeks and days of her life.

The hurdles her future still presented.

Even the weight of responsibility she had to keep her family safe and happy.

Good grief…it had only been a matter of hours ago that she had made the firm resolution not to let her own desire to be near Jack interfere with those responsibilities to her family, and look what one kiss had done.

Jack looked as bemused as she was by the scene in the kitchen. Dougal's pawprints led all the way to his bed in the corner now. He picked up his bedraggled duck toy and trotted back to drop the offering at Jack's feet. She saw him slowly close his eyes as if he needed to find strength.

'I'll put the kettle on, shall I?' she heard herself ask faintly.

Somehow, over the time it took to give everybody a hot drink, a semblance of order returned.

'How are you feeling?' Jack asked Kerry. 'No more contractions?'

'Not yet.'

'Contractions?' Barnaby looked awestruck. 'You're not...I mean...when is your baby due?'

'I almost had it yesterday,' Kerry told him.

'No-o-o...'

'Could be any time, I guess,' she continued cheerfully. 'You've probably got a better idea than me, what with you being so psychic and everything.'

'I'm not sick,' Holly announced. 'I'm *hungry*.'

'Ooh...food.' Barnaby riffled through the catalogues. 'That's something else we need to think about for Christmas.'

'We might need something a little sooner than that.' It was a relief for Lizzie to have something practical to focus on but why hadn't she thought to drop in at a supermarket on the way here?

Oh...yes... She hadn't intended for them to still be here at dinnertime, had she?

'Let me take care of that.' Jack stood up quickly. 'We've got a few good shops in the village. Anyone got any objections to fish and chips?'

'Are you kidding?' Kerry beamed at him. 'I come from New Zealand. That's our national dish, mate.'

'My favourite, too,' Barnaby sighed. 'But I'll be in deep strife if I go AWOL with the shop's truck any longer.' He turned from Kerry to Jack. 'Do you want me to unload the tree and stuff?'

Jack looked at Lizzie and she saw a flash of, what... apology? Hope?

'I ordered some decorations and things online,' he explained belatedly. 'I thought that you might all...like to spend your Christmas here.'

'I picked the best,' Barnaby assured Jack. 'I got the biggest, most realistic tree there is and there's *eight* different programmes on how you can make the lights twinkle. Sparkling, chasing, my personal favourite slow-glow...' He trailed off, his gaze going from Lizzie to Jack and back again.

'I think that's the nicest thing anybody's ever done,' Kerry said mistily. 'Christmas in a truck.'

'For me, too?' Holly's whisper could be heard because the room had gone so quiet. 'And...and Misty?'

Jack crouched to her level. 'Especially for you,' he said softly. He looked up at Lizzie. 'If it's OK with Mummy?'

Lizzie couldn't find any words. She couldn't even find a coherent thought. She heard the softness in Jack's voice and watched his lips move and all she could do was relive the way his kiss had made her feel.

Helpless to do anything else, she nodded her head and managed a rather wobbly smile.

Jack didn't want to go home.

There was no real reason t stay any longer, however. He'd provided food and stayed to share it. Holly had gone to bed and so had Kerry.

'They told me at St Bethel's to get lots of rest,' she'd excused herself. 'See you tomorrow, Jack.'

Except she wouldn't if he went back to his apartment. As he should do.

As he *was* doing.

Lizzie was seeing him out. 'Dougal could do with some fresh air,' she said. 'And I'd better made sure he stays off that rose garden.'

The boxes from the Bennett's truck were stacked in the front entranceway. Boxes of all shapes and sizes, including an extraordinarily long one.

'That tree...' Jack stopped to look at the box. 'I should help you unpack it.' He saw Lizzie open her mouth to protest but he was already shrugging his coat off again. 'You're still recuperating from surgery,' he reminded Lizzie. 'And Kerry could go into proper labour any time soon. This thing looks like it weighs a ton.'

In actual fact, it was remarkably light. The tree came in sections that fitted together, with a sturdy base to keep it upright and stable. The branches were folded against the trunk and there were smaller branches and then twigs that had wire inside so that they could be straightened and fluffed out into a real tree shape. Jack had to go out into snow that was falling quite heavily and unearth a ladder from the barn to fit the top sections in place. Lizzie was allowed to unfurl branches and twigs.

'It's huge,' she said. 'And so real looking. It even *smells* like a spruce.'

'I'm just glad it's green and not blue,' Jack said. 'Let's find those lights Barnaby was raving about. And some decorations. This tree is rather high and I can't let you or Kerry climb around on ladders.'

The lights came on netting and it took a while to lay it out and then it drape around the tree. And then, of course, they had to plug it in and test it. Jack turned out the main lights in the room and picked up the remote control, scrolling through the options.

'"Sparkling" is a bit frenetic, isn't it?'

Hundreds—possibly thousands—of fairy-lights were flashing on and off at speed and having a kind of strobe effect.

'Chasing' was better but still busy.

'Slow glow' made the tree black and then pinpricks of light slowly brightened until it glowed steadily all over and then they faded away again. As the light returned, Jack found himself watching Lizzie's face instead of the tree. Her eyes were as bright as the lights and she was smiling. What if he waited for the glow to start dimming and then leaned over and kissed her again?

'Nice,' Lizzie murmured appreciatively.

Oh…it would be. More than nice. But would they stop with a kiss? How could he even be thinking of anything more with a woman who was still recovering from some fairly major abdominal surgery?

A woman who was, first and foremost, a mother?

A woman who had a heart as big as Texas, who could love easily and completely. Who could have her heart broken.

Jack hurriedly clicked the remote. 'This is "Twinkle".'

'Twinkle' was perfect. Less romantic. Pretty and quintessentially Christmas, but Jack turned it off.

'I'll put the main lights on again,' he said, 'so I can do the decorations for the top of the tree at least. You and Holly can do the bottom tomorrow, maybe.'

He brought in box after box of the ornaments Barnaby had chosen. There were stars and balls and icicles in bright, primary colours as well as gold and silver. There were small Santas and wooden soldiers and angels and reindeer. Fruit of every kind and even tiny teddy bears and gingerbread men. And long, long garlands of gold stars and silver beads.

Lizzie unpacked and sorted things and passed them to Jack who threaded loops over twigs and branches.

'Just as well I trained as a surgeon,' he said. 'This requires a surprising amount of finesse.'

'It's looking wonderful,' Lizzie assured him. 'This room is just made for a tree like this.'

They had chosen the large drawing room of the house with its vast fireplace that could be lit on the day. The French doors would offer a view of the garden which, given the current weather conditions, would probably be like a winter picture postcard.

'It is, isn't it? Not that I've ever seen one in here before. My mother hated the cold. She always went to spend winter somewhere tropical.'

'So you had sunny Christmases? Like Kerry usually does?'

'No. I stayed in Paris with my father. Sometimes we didn't celebrate it at all. He was a very busy man and often on call on holidays.'

The reminder of how lonely a Christmas could be for a child was poignant. It wouldn't be like that for Holly and Misty. Not this year.

'He was a doctor?'

'An orthopaedic surgeon who specialised in hands.'

He could hear both hesitation and curiosity in Lizzie's voice. 'And your mother?'

'She was a model. She met my father when she was in Paris just starting her career. She left him when I was three years old, to live with her photographer. This was *her* parents' home that she inherited and they used it as a base. She sent for me occasionally, until they were both killed in an accident in South America when I was about fourteen.'

What was he doing, spilling information about his less than happy childhood? He'd never told anybody about it, even Celine. But Lizzie's warmth invited confidence. More than that. It was as if she deserved to know why he was so drawn to her and why he couldn't allow himself to act on his attraction to her.

He hung a shiny, green apple on the tree top.

'I brought my wife here once,' he said quietly. 'She hated the place.'

There was a long silence. Long enough for him to wrap the wires of half a dozen red cherries, scattering them around the smallest section of the tree.

'You're still married?'

'No. Long since divorced.' Jack didn't look down from his task. 'I learned my lesson. My job and marriage are not compatible. I'm sure you can understand. You were married to a man who served others. Heroically. It can't have been easy at times.'

'No.' The word wobbled and suddenly Jack had no desire to pursue this conversation. He'd said as much as he needed to. He didn't want to hear about how happy her marriage had been or how much she missed the twins' father.

Knowing that Jack had been married was a shock.

A piece of the puzzle that was Jack fell into place, however. On some level, she'd known there had to be a very good reason for the way he'd beaten himself up over what had happened when Holly had been in his care. Had he had to leave his wife, perhaps? Too often or on too important an occasion?

She'd been on the verge of telling him the real story of her marriage. Of saying that a job that involved being on call for when others needed you might be an inconvenience but it was never enough on its own to destroy a marriage. Hers hadn't been easy for other reasons. She'd married a man who had lived only for the thrill of his job. A wife and especially children had been an inconvenience. But maybe that was how Jack felt about his work? Did she really want to go there?

There were other thoughts pushing into her head. What Jack had said, or rather what he hadn't said, about his childhood. Had he ever had a real, family Christmas? Was that need what this was really all about? Deep in thought, she reached into a new box.

'There's the most gorgeous star here.' She held it up. 'Do you think it should go on the top of the tree?'

It was huge, with long points. Snowy white with an intricate pattern of silver and gold glitter.

'I think it should,' Jack said gravely. He came down the ladder a couple of rungs to take it from her. 'And then we'll be finished decorating the top of the tree and we'll be done for the night.'

Would they?

Lizzie was caught by Jack's gaze. By the way his hand was touching hers as he took the star.

Had they stepped over some kind of barrier just now? Taken steps towards understanding each other?

Loving each other, maybe?

Jack attached the star to the very top of the tree and then came down off the ladder so that he was standing beside Lizzie. For a moment, they both admired the work in progress. And then they turned to look at each other.

'It's getting late,' Jack said. 'And by the look of the weather out there, I might be stuck until Jimmy gets here with the shovel in the morning.'

'You could stay here,' Lizzie said. 'There are any number of bedrooms.'

'I could.' But Jack looked doubtful.

'You'll be here for Christmas, won't you?' It was more of a plea than a query.

She could see the way Jack drew in a deep breath. 'Do you want me to be?'

'Oh…yes.' Of course she wanted him to be here.

She wanted *him*. So much that it hurt.

'Then I will be here,' Jack said. His gaze held hers.

'Just for Christmas, Lizzie.' Bending his head, he kissed her softly.

Was he saying they could have this time together? As a gift?

It wasn't enough. It could never be enough but it was infinitely preferable to not having any of Jack at all.

It would have to be enough. Lizzie stood on tiptoe to return the kiss with one of her own.

'We'll just have to make the most of every moment of Christmas, then, won't we?'

Starting tonight. She was more than recovered enough to be close to a man she knew would be capable of being very gentle. She hoped she could convey that message with the look they were sharing. With another kiss.

It seemed to work. Jack took hold of her hand and led her upstairs.

CHAPTER ELEVEN

Two days later, Maggie came out of hospital.

Not only was the tree completely decorated by then, but there was mile after mile of tinsel throughout the house. Every doorknob was adorned and the banister rails entwined. A huge wreath, bright with holly berries, was attached to the big front door.

Jimmy, the groundsman, had been co-opted into moving a bed downstairs, into a smaller living area near the kitchen and an old, but perfectly serviceable guest bathroom. He drew the line at weaving fairy lights through the bare branches of the trees in the garden, however.

'Ne'er heard such nonsense in m' life,' he grumbled.

Lizzie simply smiled at him. It was quite clear by now that Jimmy had a heart of gold beneath his gruff exterior. He'd been a frequent presence since the day he'd discovered her with Jack in the garden. He found an endless list of jobs that needed doing, like shovelling snow and chopping and hauling firewood. Even burning hedge clippings out behind the barn. Whatever he was doing outside, Dougal was now his faithful companion. The Matthews' exuberant dog had never been so well behaved in his life, desperately eager for the tiniest hint of approval from the giant man who had arrived in their lives. Right now, he was sitting, ramrod straight, beside Jimmy as the older man watched Maggie climb gingerly from the car.

Lizzie was ready with the crutches.

'Not too many stairs, Mum. Not like at home, when the lifts aren't working, that's for sure.'

Funny how it sounded odd referring to their apartment as 'home'. While Lizzie knew all too well that it would cause her considerable grief in the not-too-distant future, her heart was here. In this wonderful old country house that was beginning to sparkle with Christmas joy. *Jack's* house…

Maggie took the crutches and positioned her hands. 'I don't know about this at all,' she muttered. 'Having Christmas in someone else's house. A *stranger's* house.'

'Jack's not a stranger, Mum. He's…'

The most wonderful man she could ever meet. Clever, kind, generous to a fault. *Passionate*…

'He's a friend,' she finished hurriedly, feeling her mother's keen gaze.

'Oh-h…*friends*, now, is it?' But Maggie's attention was suddenly diverted as she caught sight of Jimmy and Dougal standing nearby. She suddenly seemed to have a moment of difficulty keeping her balance with the crutches.

'This is Jimmy, Mum. He looks after this place for Jack. He lives in the old gamekeeper's cottage on the other side of the lake.'

'James McDuff,' Jimmy said formally. 'Pleasure, ma'am.'

'Heavens above.' Maggie blinked. 'You make me sound like royalty.'

She gripped her crutches firmly and moved carefully to the wide stone steps that Jimmy had shovelled and swept snow from more than once today.

He was watching as Maggie got the first step and paused, clearly going over the instructions from the physiotherapist about how to tackle such an obstacle.

Jimmy stepped closer. 'I dinna think you should be doing that, lass,' he said. 'I canna guarantee these blithering steps aren't as slippery as a sheet o' ice. Here...' Without asking for any kind of permission, he took the crutches from Maggie and handed them to a startled Lizzie. Then he gently scooped Maggie into his arms and carried her into the house.

'Oh, my goodness...' Maggie's voice was rather faint. 'Where are you taking me?'

'Bed,' Jimmy growled, obviously uncomfortable being inside the house. 'I'm taking you to bed, woman.'

Lizzie could only follow behind, stifling a giggle and carrying the crutches and Maggie's small bag. She indulged in a small fantasy of being scooped up in a similar fashion by Jack and having him say something very similar, preferably in French.

That was the language he preferred, she'd discovered, when it came to the bedroom.

Such a beautiful language. She might not understand the words but the gentle touches and searingly hot kisses that came with them made the sounds more exciting than anything she'd ever heard.

Jack had been *so* gentle that first night but she'd been fine. The night after that she had spent in the hospital with Misty but last night she'd been treated to a glimpse of what his love-making could be like when she was completely healed again and the whisper of barely contained passion had taken her breath away.

Would he be around long enough for her to discover the full depth of where that passion could take them?

Would he be around tonight, even, with her mother now in the house as well?

Jimmy certainly wasn't going to hang around inside for a moment longer than he had to. He was an outside man, through and through.

Maggie settled back against the pillows on her bed, staring at the door Jimmy had disappeared through. She was blinking like an owl.

'He called me *lass*,' she said to Lizzie. 'For heaven's sake, he can't be any older than I am and he made me feel like...like a girl.'

'It's a Scottish thing.' Lizzie smiled. 'And don't take any notice of his grumpiness. Jack said he was terrified of him when he was Holly's age but he's a lovely man, really. Apparently he adored his wife. She died about twenty years ago but he's never got over it.'

'That's sad,' was all Maggie said. 'Where *is* Holly? And Kerry, for that matter?'

'Holly's in the kitchen, trying to finish her "welcome home" card for you. I'll go and get her. Kerry's at Bennett's. Shopping.'

'Again? I hope you're keeping an eye on how much that girl is spending.'

'I suspect part of the lure is the supervision she's getting from young Barnaby. And I don't think I've got much to say about how much is being spent, Mum. This is Jack's doing. He's making Christmas, for all of us.'

Maggie gave her daughter a long look. 'I hope you know what *you're* doing, love.'

Lizzie nodded with more confidence than she felt. 'It's just for Christmas,' she said quietly. 'We're all going to make the most of it for as long as it lasts.' She lifted her chin. 'And then normal life will resume but… but we'll all have something wonderful to remember.'

'Hmm…' Maggie's eyes might be troubled but her smile was full of love. 'I could do with a cup of tea,' she said. 'And a cuddle from that granddaughter of mine.'

Kerry didn't finish all the shopping and wrapping that had to happen at Bennett's department store until three days before Christmas. Then Lizzie got a phone call on her mobile.

'Are you at home?' Kerry asked.

Lizzie was in the kitchen of Jack's house. There was a delicious smell of roasting chickens and vegetables coming from the Aga's oven.

Holly was in the 'Christmas room' as the living area with the tree was now known, happily showing her grandmother—yet again—the decorations *she* had attached to the tree all by herself.

Dougal was stretched out on the stone flags that were warmed by the stove, his paws twitching and his tail thumping occasionally, deep in a canine dream and utterly content.

Jack was on the other side of the kitchen table, pulling the cork from a chilled bottle of a very nice-looking white wine.

Lizzie closed her eyes for a heartbeat. 'Yes,' she said aloud. 'I'm at home.'

'Cool. I thought you might be in with Misty still.'

'I came home for dinner. I'm going back in later. She's got some very particular ideas about what clothes she wants to come home in tomorrow. I thought I'd spend the night in with her again. She's so excited she won't get a wink of sleep otherwise. Where are you?'

'Deep in the bowels of Bennett's. You wouldn't believe what it looks like down here. I'm absolutely sure that Santa and about a million elves are somewhere around here.'

Nelfs, Lizzie thought mistily. A smile tugged at her lips as her gaze flew to Jack.

He chose that moment to look up and it felt like he knew exactly what she was thinking.

It was all there, encapsulated in that tiny, non-existent word.

The way they'd met. The connection a small, sick girl and her twin sister had provided. The trust. The rescues that had made Jack the rock in a very traumatic period of her life. The overwhelming generosity of this man.

The overwhelming love Lizzie had for him.

Jack smiled back and, in that moment, Lizzie thought her life could never be more perfect than this.

Except that Kerry's excited voice was distracting her.

'Barney's sorting chains for the truck. Have you ever *seen* so much snow?'

Barney? Lizzie had to give herself a mental shake. 'It's amazing, isn't it? Jack's hired a four-wheel-drive thing that looks like a tank so he can make sure he can get to work. He's going to bring me and Misty home in it tomorrow.'

'Cool… Oh, hang on…'

Lizzie could hear a muffled conversation going on. Then some giggling. And then a long moment of silence. Kerry sounded distinctly breathless when she came back on the line.

'OK. We're good to go. I just needed to ring to make sure that you kept Holly somewhere she won't see the barn out the windows. We're going to stash all the presents in there and then we can put them under the tree on Christmas Eve when the girls are sound asleep. Do you happen to know if the barn door is unlocked?'

'I'll check.' Lizzie relayed the plan to Jack. 'The door will be open by the time you get here,' she informed Kerry a minute later. 'And I'll keep your dinner warm. There's enough if…um…Barney wants to stay.'

If they ate around the kitchen table, Lizzie decided, Holly would be well away from seeing the unusual arrival of a delivery truck in the dark. The ancient daybed in the corner of this farmhouse-style room would be perfect to give her mother a comfortable place to eat.

'I had to get the key for the barn from Jimmy,' Jack said when he returned. 'I asked him if he wanted some dinner but he said he'd better supervise that delivery.' Jack was grinning. 'He muttered something about "bairns with bits of silverware stuck all over their faces" and not trusting them to lock up again.'

'I'll save him some dinner too,' Lizzie said. 'There's heaps.'

Dougal heard the arrival of the truck as they were sitting down to eat. Lizzie casually let him out the back door. She knew he would go no further than where Jimmy happened to be and that his newfound hero would bring him back to the house. Dougal had followed Jimmy home to his cottage only yesterday and Lizzie had been informed that her 'blithering dog' was a pest.

Sure enough, Jimmy turned up at the back door with Dougal in tow, some time later, when Holly was attacking a bowl of chocolate ice cream for dessert.

Jack went to the door. Lizzie was rinsing dishes in the sink and couldn't hear what was being said but the agitated tone of Jimmy's voice carried all too clearly. She was drying her hands on a tea towel as she moved swiftly towards the two men. She had the horrible feeling that Dougal might be in trouble again.

But it wasn't Dougal who was in trouble.

'Call an ambulance,' Jack told her quietly. 'And then bring some towels and a blanket or two out to the barn. Sounds like Kerry's in labour for real this time.'

The barn was a building even older than the house. It stood, tucked between some centuries-old oak trees on the other side of a sympathetically built but far more modern garaging complex. Beams, blackened by time, held a slate roof at an enormous height above a cobbled floor. Ancient farm machinery and dusty hay bales lined the walls.

It was amongst these bales of hay that Barnaby and Kerry had been stowing a vast pile of brightly wrapped Christmas gifts. It was now where Kerry was lying on blankets, clutching Barnaby's hands and groaning loudly as another contraction took hold of her body.

'This isn't supposed to be happening,' she gasped when she could speak again.

'Not entirely true,' Jack said calmly from his position between Kerry's knees. 'It was always going to happen at some point in the not-too-distant future.'

'Not *now*.' Kerry's upper back and head were being supported by Barnaby's body as he knelt behind her. His arms were around the young woman, giving her both of his hands to grip. He was looking very pale.

'Not *here*,' Kerry groaned. 'In a *barn*.'

'Hey, it's almost a stable.' Lizzie was beside Jack, ready with clean towels and anything else he might need from the medical kit he'd snatched from the boot of his car. She could see the baby's head beginning to crown. 'It's very Christmas.'

'Ooh...' Kerry screwed up her face and bore down. Barnaby looked like he was bearing down in sympathy.

Moments later, it seemed, the baby emerged into Jack's hands. Kerry's arms were outstretched now, reaching for her infant, but Jack held it for just a moment longer, watching as the tiny boy took his first breath and moved those miniature limbs.

Lizzie could see how gently he held the baby. She unfolded a soft towel so they could cover the baby to place it on Kerry's skin and for just a matter of seconds they were connected. Herself and Jack and the newborn.

Only the briefest snatch of time but it was long enough to remember what it had been like to see her daughters for the first time. To remember that all-consuming love that time had only served to make stronger. Long enough to imagine what it would be like if *this* child was her own. If Jack was the father.

Such a short space of time but Lizzie knew that yearning sensation would probably be with her for ever.

Thank God the delivery had been so straightforward. Jack hadn't had any part in delivering a baby since medical school but this infant hadn't been about to wait for some more experienced assistance. At least he'd had a medical kit available, even if he had only used the gloves and something to cut the cord with later.

He stripped off the gloves as Lizzie tucked the baby against Kerry's skin and covered them both with blankets while they waited for the paramedics to arrive.

He couldn't strip off the feeling of holding that newborn baby in his hands, though. He couldn't shut his ears to the wobbly cries or his eyes to the expression on Kerry's face. Or Barnaby's or Lizzie's for that matter.

Birth *was* a miracle. A new life. This baby had an adoring, albeit very young mother. It potentially had a father figure as well, if that look of pride on Barnaby's face and the way he was staying in physical contact with Kerry was anything to go by.

What would he look like if he really was the father?

What would feel like to see your own child come into the world?

Jack had learned long ago that fatherhood would not be a part of his own future but that didn't necessarily mean that he wouldn't *want* to be a father. It just wasn't possible. Echoes of Celine's voice were readily available if he needed any reminders of why that was the case. Vicious words of how inadequate he was as a husband and how it was lucky they'd never had a child. How it was just as well his job was so important to him because it was all he'd ever have in his life and all he would be remembered for.

It was the way it had to be, Jack reminded himself.

The recent happenings in his life had disturbed the rhythm of his existence but this…this sensation of being a witness to something he could never experience himself held a note of something as dark as grief.

Something powerful, anyway. Something even more disturbing than anything else he'd had to contend with in the last days and weeks.

Jack turned away. He went to where Jimmy was outside the barn, stamping his feet against the bone chilling cold, waiting to direct the ambulance to where it was needed.

'It's a boy,' he told Jimmy. 'All's well.'

True enough, for Kerry and the baby, especially when the ambulance arrived and whisked her off to St Bethel's for a proper check-up. Also true for Lizzie and her family. Maggie was rapidly recovering from her surgery. Misty would be home tomorrow and they would all have a special, family Christmas.

But for himself?

All *would* be well, Jack told himself firmly. Christmas was only days away and then he would step back into his real life and leave these unsettling doubts and odd yearnings behind.

He could make a start even before then.

'Do you still want to go into Westbridge tonight?' he asked Lizzie as Jimmy locked the barn doors a while later, with the empty Bennett's truck now garaged inside. Barnaby had gone in the ambulance with Kerry.

She nodded. 'I promised Misty and Mum says she'll

be fine to look after things here. Holly's going to sleep downstairs with her. Mum said Jimmy had given her his phone number if she needed any help.'

An odd sound came from Jimmy, as if he was clearing his throat and growling at the same time, as he walked off into the night.

Jack merely nodded. 'I'll drive you in. I may stay in there myself. Dave's got a young patient he's got me involved with and he's getting to crisis point, I think.'

'Oh, no…a child?'

'Four-year-old boy. Liam, his name is. He's already had a whole bowel transplant but it's been failing for some time. He's been back in Intensive Care since just after Misty got out. There's very little chance of him getting a new transplant in time.'

'Oh-h…' Lizzie looked stricken. 'That poor family. They're going to lose their little boy? At Christmastime?'

'Quite likely.' Again, Jack had to turn away from something overpoweringly emotional. 'Are you ready to leave?'

Lizzie was very quiet on the long drive into the city that night. They went their separate ways as they reached the foyer of the hospital. Lizzie was clutching the bag that contained Misty's clothes for the next day but she stood on tiptoe and planted a soft kiss on Jack's cheek. He could see tears in her eyes.

'I'm so lucky,' she whispered. 'Aren't I?'

Jack watched as she walked away to be with her child who was no longer sick, knowing that she could be content in the knowledge that the rest of her family, including Kerry and the new baby, were all safe. That they would all be together again very soon. In time to celebrate Christmas.

She was indeed lucky. Blessed, in fact.

If Jack could choose the family he would most want to have as his own, it would be this one.

But even he couldn't really belong, it didn't have to stop him caring about them, did it?

This way, he was getting to show them how much he did care. About all of them, but especially Lizzie.

And this way, they would never be let down by him. He would never have to see disappointment or the anger of betrayal in Lizzie's eyes when she learned how impossible it was for him to be more than a friend.

It had to be this way. For all their sakes. For himself, for Lizzie and for two little girls who needed a devoted, full-time father.

The thought was supposed to be comforting him that he was doing the right thing by everybody but the heavy feeling in Jack's chest wouldn't go away. It got worse, if anything, as he made his way towards the paediatric intensive care unit. To spend his night with a small patient he knew he was most unlikely to be able to save.

That weight was still there the next day. Caught up with the surgery Liam needed to remove another piece of his failing bowel, Jack had to arrange a car to take Lizzie and Misty home. He stayed in the city that night as well, after it became likely that Liam could be rushed back to Theatre at any time. The young boy's condition had stabilised overnight, however.

'Take a break,' Dave Kingsley advised, later that

morning. 'It's Christmas Eve. Go home, Jack. I'll call you if anything changes.'

A change couldn't possibly be good. Unless...

It *was* Christmas. Maybe there was a miracle waiting to happen for Liam. Except that if it did happen, it would mean tragedy for a different family.

Life was a curious balance, Jack decided as he drove away from the hospital. Life and death. Joy and sadness. You could only do the best you could for the people you had the chance to care about.

And maybe that was why he automatically took the route away from the central city. Towards the place where he knew some Christmas magic was already happening.

The blanket of snow got thicker and softer as Jack got closer to the villages on the outskirts of London. Someone on the radio was telling him that the weather this year was breaking all manner of records. The whole of the British Isles would be having their whitest Christmas in decades.

The main roads were being kept reasonably clear and he knew that Jimmy was making sure the long driveway of the country estate was passable.

Lizzie had told him that, last night, when he'd rung to apologise for not being able to drive her home, as promised. He'd been listening for a note of disappointment in her voice because he'd let her down but she brushed off the apology.

'It was brilliant having the car again. Kerry and the baby were both given glowing reports and allowed to come home so, I hope you don't mind, I sent the car to fetch them.'

Of course he didn't mind but he was only half listening as Lizzie went on to tell him that Barnaby had arrived with a bassinet and baby supplies when he'd come back to retrieve the truck. He was too busy trying to analyse his strange reaction to Lizzie's acceptance of his inability to keep a promise.

Had she been prepared for it?

Did it not really matter to her?

Maybe he needed it to matter. For Lizzie to understand why the rules in his life couldn't be broken.

Even for her…

He hadn't come any closer to figuring it out when he finally reached the house in the early hours of the afternoon. The snow had stopped falling some time back during his journey and between the vast, cotton-wool balls of cloud a weak sun was making an appearance. It was still a surprise, however, to see so many people outside the house.

The twins were on the lawn, the snow almost level with the tops of their gumboots. They were buttoned up in anoraks and had mittens on their hands. Their heads were covered with woollen hats that left only their wide eyes and joyous smiles exposed.

Identical faces. With astonishment, Jack realised that this was the first time he'd seen the twins standing side by side. A complete set.

'We're going to make a *snowman*,' Holly shouted gleefully as Jack stepped out of the car.

'Just a small one.' Lizzie was also wrapped up well against the cold. She had a cherry-red knitted hat over her curls and her cheeks were almost the same colour.

'Misty's been cooped up in hospital rooms for so long, I didn't think a bit of fresh air would do her any harm.'

Her smile was as joyous as the ones on her daughters' faces and no wonder... Here she was, with two healthy, happy little girls, about to embark on a such a traditional, family activity.

The longing to be a part of it was too strong to resist. Letting his gaze hold Lizzie's for long enough to be far more than merely a greeting was just as irresistible.

This was a moment of joy, Jack realised. Part of the balance of life and exactly what he needed after the gruelling time talking to Liam's family this morning.

He didn't even need to ask. Lizzie's eyes were smiling. 'We could use some help. I don't want Misty out here for too long.'

Jack pulled his leather gloves from the pocket of his coat. A peal of laughter from the girls made him look up to see that Dougal was trying to run in the garden but the snow was so deep in places that he was having to bound along like a small kangaroo. He was staying within range of Jimmy, who had a very long ladder tucked under one arm.

'I canna believe I let Margaret talk me into this,' he grumbled as he marched past Jack towards where Maggie was standing beneath a tree, her crutches looking out of place on either side of snow-encrusted gumboots.. 'Lights in trees. Ne'er heard such nonsense.'

Jack and Lizzie shared a grin and the bubble of joy got bigger. Jack scooped up a handful of snow and patted it into a ball.

'Help me roll this,' he invited the twins. 'We can use it to make the snowman's tummy.'

Only Misty was paying attention as Jack demonstrated how to enlarge the snowball quickly. Holly was lying on her back, waving her arms and legs to make a snow angel.

'Look at me, Mummy. *Oof...* Dougal—get off. *Bad dog.*'

Jimmy looked down from the top of the ladder, a long string of coloured lights in his hands.

'Get out of it, dog,' he commanded.

Dougal leapt up, shook snow off his coat and slunk away, looking suitably chastened. Holly also got up and went to help Misty roll the snowball.

The snowman took on an odd shape as the twins scooped more and more snow and patted it around the base of the main ball. The middle ball became far too small and when Jack tried to position the head, it slipped off and broke.

'He's got no *head*,' Holly wailed.

Misty's eyes were huge. And sad. 'It doesn't look like a real snowman,' she said.

'Hmm.' Jack's tone was thoughtful. 'You know what? It looks like a snow *dog*.'

Lizzie's smile was all the encouragement he needed. 'Look...we can give him paws here...and ears there...' His gloves were soggy with melted snow and his hands were cold but it didn't matter in the least. 'All he needs now are some eyes and a nose. Can you find some stones on the driveway?'

But neither of the twins was listening.

'Where *is* Dougal?' Misty asked anxiously.

Lizzie sounded equally worried. 'I haven't seen him

since Jimmy told him off for wrecking Holly's snow angel.'

Jimmy was still up the ladder, onto his third tree now.

'James?' Maggie was keeping the base of the ladder steady. 'Can you see where Dougal is?'

The string of lights stopped moving. A moment later, Jimmy's voice floated down from the tree, heavy with disapproval.

'Idiot dog's out on the pond.' His voice rose to a roar. '*Dog*...Come *here*.'

Looking in the right direction now, Jack could see Dougal across the smooth expanse of snow covering the small lake. He must have made his way around the edge to get there but, in his eagerness to obey Jimmy's command, he was now bounding straight across the middle.

'Oh...*no*...'

Lizzie's head swivelled at his tone. So did Maggie's and the little girls'. They all heard the crack of thin ice and saw the moment that Dougal vanished. They all heard the dog's terrified yelp.

Jack looked at the fear in their faces. Dougal was a much-loved pet.

He had to *do* something. He had to fix this for them.

Aware of nothing but the need to protect every member of this family—*his* family—Jack walked out onto the ice. He ignored the shout that came from Jimmy as the older man descended from the tree at speed.

He wasn't being a 'blithering idiot'. He was testing each footfall and listening for the warning sound of ice that was too thin to take his weight. He'd even grabbed

a long branch of dead wood, although he wasn't sure
how helpful it was going to be.

He could see Dougal floundering in the icy water,
desperately trying to haul himself out, but the edges of
the ice were breaking away in chunks. The dog's heavy
coat was waterlogged and he had to be getting very cold
very fast. It would only be a matter of a minute or two
until any energy he had to save himself would be gone.

Jack was closer now. Almost close enough to touch
Dougal with the branch.

That was when he heard the ice starting to crack.

When he heard the fear in Lizzie's voice behind him.

'Jack...'

CHAPTER TWELVE

THE horror of hearing that ice cracking would haunt Lizzie for ever.

Two small girls were clutching at her and she had to crouch down and draw them both closer. Had to bow her head as the fear hit her that she might be about to lose Jack in a way she wasn't the tiniest bit prepared for.

In a way there would be no going back from.

'It's all right, love.' Her mother's voice came with a touch of her hands on Lizzie's shoulders. 'James has the ladder down. Jack's safe. He's using the ladder to reach Dougal.'

The twins sobbed more loudly at the mention of their pet's name. They were still sobbing when Dougal was brought back to them, a sodden, violently shivering and utterly miserable bundle in Jimmy's arms.

'He's a stupid dog,' Jimmy informed them, but his tone lacked any rancour. 'And he needs a hot bath. I'm going to take him to my house.'

'I'll come and help,' Maggie offered instantly.

'We want to help, too,' Holly sobbed. Misty grabbed

her sister's hand and nodded, tears still streaming down her cheeks.

Jimmy looked at the twins. Then he looked at Maggie and his face softened into the first real smile Lizzie had ever seen him give.

'Aye…come on, then, the lot o' you.'

Lizzie had to go with them, of course. Misty, especially, needed to be watched that she wasn't overdoing things and she could swear there'd been an unspoken conversation going on between her mother and Jack's burly groundsman that was both startling and a bit… wonderful.

Not that she was capable of feeling anything joyful right now. She was still shaking herself and it had nothing at all to do with the cold. She hung back as the small procession set off towards Jimmy's cottage.

'*Why?*' she had to ask. 'Why did you *do* that, Jack?'

He looked taken aback by the vehemence in her voice.

'I wanted to rescue Dougal,' he said. 'For the girls. For *you*. What sort of Christmas would if have been if anything had happened to the pet they love?'

Lizzie shook her head sharply, struggling to keep tears at bay.

'You wanted to be a hero,' she choked out accusingly. 'I know about heroes, remember? I was married to one.'

Jack's face emptied of any expression. 'Yes…you were.'

'You put *yourself* in danger,' Lizzie continued brokenly. 'Did you stop to think about what Christmas would have been like if something had happened to

you? How would Holly and Misty have felt about that?
And Jimmy, for that matter. And Maggie and Kerry
and Barney and…and me.' She had to turn away. 'The
people that *love* you?'

Jack wasn't saying anything and Lizzie couldn't turn
back to look at him. She'd just confessed her love to
a man who'd made it very clear he could be nothing
more than a friend. That whatever they had here—all
of them—was only for Christmas.

'Mummy.' Holly's call was urgent. 'Hurry up.
Dougal's *wet*.'

Lizzie's face was also wet. She couldn't let Jack she
how broken she felt right now. Not after all he'd done
for them. She couldn't let her family see either.

Scrubbing at her face, she hurried.

For the longest time, Jack simply stood there, watching
the small knot of people disappear into the trees on the
path that led to the cottage.

They didn't need his help. Jimmy would run a bath
and warm Dougal and then dry him in front of the
fire, probably with the help of the three generations of
Lizzie's family and a lot of old towels.

Not being needed was disappointing but it wasn't
what was creating this churning in his gut.

Lizzie thought he'd been trying to be some kind of
hero. Like the twins' father had been. And she was
upset. Because she was reminded of how she'd lost the
man she'd loved?

But she'd said she loved *him*.

That they *all* loved him.

There was a very strange prickling sensation happening behind his eyes and his throat felt too tight to swallow.

A sense of loss, that's what it was.

That he was facing the loss of something so important it was turning his whole life inside out. Something just as important—maybe *more* important—than the career he loved with such a passion.

Mon Dieu.

Even his marriage to Celine had never presented a conflict like this.

Maybe he'd always known, deep down, that loving anybody like this would create this tearing feeling of divided loyalty. Maybe that was why he'd never loved anybody this much.

Or perhaps it was simply because he'd never met Lizzie Matthews.

It was a hopeless situation. He couldn't compromise his work because that was who he *was*.

Lizzie had been married to someone who'd felt the same way about his career and she'd suffered heartbreak because of it. She was strong and independent now. She didn't need him in her life any more than they'd needed him to help look after Dougal.

Jack felt curiously lost.

If he went inside the house, he would be with Kerry and her new baby and that could only make him more aware of what he was missing in his own life.

He needed dry clothes. The chill was rapidly closing in on his bones. Heating his vehicle would keep him comfortable until he got to his apartment. There were other things he could do today as well. He could check up on Liam's condition and remind himself of the career that was waiting to enfold and comfort him in the near future.

As he drove away, leaving the house and cottage and all the people they contained well behind, another idea began to take shape in Jack's mind.

Shops would be open until late tonight with it being Christmas Eve. Bennett's was probably open until midnight. Kerry had been tasked with finding presents for Lizzie and Maggie but the emphasis had been on Holly and Misty. And it hadn't occurred to him to try and find a gift that he could give Lizzie himself.

What if he could find something that would let her know how much he cared? Something that she could keep and treasure for ever?

Diamonds were for ever. Yes…that would be perfect. A beautiful necklace, maybe. Or a bracelet.

Something with diamonds and a sapphire.

Because he'd never see a sapphire again himself, without being reminded of the colour of Lizzie's eyes.

Lizzie had to draw on every ounce of courage and independence she possessed when she discovered that Jack had simply disappeared when they returned to the house with a still subdued but dry Dougal.

'He probably got called into the hospital,' Maggie said. 'He'll be back tomorrow. He said he wouldn't want to miss my Christmas dinner.'

It was a long evening, waiting for a phone call that didn't happen. Even the twins' excitement at putting out a glass of milk and a gingerbread cookie for Father Christmas couldn't melt the heaviness in Lizzie's heart. She finally got the twins settled, but only after giving in to the pleas that Dougal could be allowed to sleep on the floor between their beds as a special treat after his ordeal.

Lizzie had an ordeal of her own to deal with. One that she knew was very likely to keep her awake all night. She'd told Jack she loved him and he'd vanished. Part of her dreaded seeing him again.

A bigger part of her desperately wanted to.

Late that night, when they were sure the twins were soundly asleep, Maggie took charge of watching the still-nameless baby while Kerry and Lizzie ferried beautifully wrapped parcels from the barn to put under the Christmas tree.

Most of the gifts were labelled for Holly and Misty but Lizzie saw one labelled for herself. There was one for Maggie as well. Even some for Dougal, the size of one suggesting it had to be a new bed.

'I know nothing,' Kerry insisted, with a broad grin. 'I'm an elf who can keep a secret.'

She wasn't the only one, Lizzie mused as she stuffed the felt stockings Maggie had made with the small items she'd found in the hospital gift shop and then hung them over the fireplace. Would she ever find out what Holly had asked Father Christmas for, that day?

The Christmas room was now out of bounds until to-morrow afternoon because the tradition in the Matthews household was that the morning was for birthdays and the afternoon for Christmas.

There was always a bit of mixing up in the celebra-tions and that had become traditional, too. Like sing-ing 'Merry birthday to you' as they shared a breakfast of Maggie's famous pancakes and a birthday cake.

The gifts for the birthdays had been sorted well before any of the recent dramas in their lives and Lizzie was grateful she'd kept it simple, with pretty new dresses and shoes and cardigans that had been knitted by their nanna, with love. There was always a danger of over-doing things with a combined Christmas and birthday and the huge pile of gifts under the tree worried her that this year was setting a precedent that she would never be able to live up to.

Along with Jack, Jimmy had been invited to join the family for Christmas dinner. Barnaby had invited him-self.

'Professional development,' he'd cited. 'I need to gauge customer satisfaction.'

Maggie insisted on being in charge of the kitchen. She was as fit as a fiddle, she claimed, down to using only one crutch and that would be gone in a week or two.

The turkey and vegetables were roasting and the bread sauce had been made. Brussel sprouts were wait-ing in their pot, much to twins' disgust. Plum pudding and the pavlova Kerry insisted was essential were ready for later and the beautifully decorated ham was resplen-dent on the formal dining table that had been set with the antique silverware and crystal glasses they'd found in the sideboard. The table had a lovely centrepiece Maggie had created from branches of holly and some real mistletoe.

'James found the mistletoe for me,' she said.

'Did he kiss you?' Kerry laughed.

Maggie smiled. 'Maybe.'

'*Mum...*' But Lizzie didn't get the chance to interrogate her mother. Their guests were arriving.

Jimmy came up the drive at the same time as Jack was pulling in to park, with Barnaby in his passenger seat. Jimmy cut an impressive figure in his Sunday-best kilt, his hair sleekly combed and his knee high white socks a blinding white, but Lizzie only had eyes for Jack. He was also well dressed but what he was wearing didn't matter at all, it was the expression on his face that caught Lizzie.

It was tender. A bit sad, maybe. But his smile was as gorgeous as it had ever been and it had a warmth that had Lizzie flying down the steps to hug him. Jack bent his head and brushed her lips with his.

'You look...*absolument magnifique, ma chérie.*'

The words were so soft. Intimate. Nobody else could hear them but Maggie had emerged from the house in time to see how close together they were standing.

'Oh, my goodness,' she murmured. 'Like that now, is it?' And then she caught sight of Jimmy and was rendered speechless.

Jimmy seemed to be equally lost for words and Jack smiled.

'Give us a hand with this box,' he requested. 'Barney helped me get it into the car last night. It's not that heavy. Just a bit awkward.'

The seats in the back of the four-wheel-drive vehicle had been laid flat to accommodate an enormous box, wrapped in Christmas paper with an oversized bow attached to the top.

Lizzie's jaw dropped. There was already way too much waiting for her children. Jack saw her expression.

'It's for the girls,' he said. 'I just happened to come across it and I thought…'

He didn't get time to finish. The girls had come to the door to see what was happening. They rushed down the steps like two butterflies in their new party dresses and shoes.

'Father Christmas came,' they chorused, each grabbing one of Jack's hands. 'Come and *see*.'

It was left to Jimmy and Barnaby to manoeuvre the giant box. They got it as far as the hallway and then, somehow, the whole family got drawn into the Christmas room and it was forgotten.

Kerry and Barnaby had made brilliant choices for gifts. There were bright backpacks and pencil cases and lunch boxes that let the girls know they would soon be back at school. Together. There were books and DVDs to share and games that needed more than one player. For Lizzie, there was a beautiful photo frame.

'For a *family* photo.' Kerry beamed.

There was a sewing kit for Maggie. And lots of Bennett's shortbread.

There was a stuffed hedgehog toy for Kerry. 'Holly told me how much you love hedgehogs,' Barnaby said shyly. 'I sneaked it in when you weren't looking.'

Dougal wasn't at all interested in his new bed but the replacement duck toy that still had a squeaker was a great hit. He squeaked, everybody laughed and the sound blended perfectly with the Christmas carols playing in the background.

It was Barnaby who came up with the most innovative gift.

'Noel,' he said loudly, after the long chorus of one of the carols.

'*Oui*,' Jack nodded. '*Joyeux Noel*. Happy Christmas.'

'No...' Barnaby looked down to where Kerry was feeding her baby as she sat beside him. 'I meant as a name.'

'Noel?' Kerry blinked. 'That's different.'

'Very Christmas,' Lizzie grinned. 'Goes with being born in almost a stable.'

'I like it,' Kerry declared. 'I really like it. Barney, you're a genius.'

'Goes with being psychic,' Barnaby said modestly.

'Yes,' Holly shouted. 'A Christmas name like me and Misty.'

'For misty-toe,' Jack murmured.

Lizzie's gaze flew to his. Where had he heard that? He leaned close. 'It's what Holly told Father Christmas,' he whispered.

'Are you going to tell me what else she said to him?'

'Maybe.' His eyes held hers. 'I believe there could be some dispensations for nelf law when it's actually Christmas Day.'

Maggie warned them that dinner would be ready very soon and that was when the box in the hallway got remembered. The twins were too overcome to unwrap it, so Lizzie did it for them. Very carefully. The flaps of the box were on the side so they could be opened like doors.

Inside, was the most beautiful dolls' house Lizzie had ever seen.

'They don't have one already, do they?' Jack whispered anxiously.

Lizzie could only shake her head. Even if they did, it would be nothing like this. A three-storied house that even had a slate roof and chimneys.

The men eased the house from the box and carried it into the Christmas room to place it near the softly crackling fire.

'You can have a peek,' Maggie said, 'but you can't play with it until after dinner.'

The back of the house opened like shutters. Some of the furniture had been displaced by movement and after the first, tentative touch, the girls were totally enthralled.

'Look, Misty…there's little cups and plates for the table.'

'There's a baby and it's got a pram.'

'Oh….*look*! There's two little girl dolls and they look just the same.'

The adults were all gathered nearby, watching. Lizzie could feel tears gathering. 'There are *twin* dolls?' she whispered to Jack.

'That's what caught *my* eye.'

There was a moment of worry when the smiles faded from the girls' faces. When they both reached into the house and picked up more of the dolls'-house family.

'This is the mummy,' Holly said to Misty.

'And this is the daddy,' Misty whispered.

For a long moment, the children stared at each other, doing that silent twin communication thing that Lizzie was well used to.

Then they both turned to look at Jack.

And they both smiled.

Maggie cleared her throat. 'Come on,' she ordered

the children. 'The sooner you eat, the sooner you can come back and play. James, can I get you to come and carve the ham, please?'

Kerry, carrying little Noel, and Barnaby trailed after the others. Even Dougal left with the duck toy clamped in his jaws but Lizzie couldn't move.

Not when Jack was still standing beside her.

'That was the most amazing gift you could ever have given them,' she said. 'Did you see that they've taken all the dolls with them?'

He had seen. They'd taken the whole family, including the daddy, and he hadn't missed the significance of the look they'd given him. Suddenly, that look they'd both bestowed on him the first day he'd met them made perfect sense.

They wanted a daddy for their own family.

They had chosen *him*.

Jack's heart rate picked up. His mouth felt curiously dry. 'I have a gift for you, Lizzie.'

'You've already given me far too much. I don't...' Lizzie's voice trailed into silence as she saw him taking the small box from the pocket of his jacket.

'I went into Bennett's yesterday,' he told her. 'I wanted to find a gift that was special enough to let you know how much I care about you. About *all* of you, of course, but *especially* you.'

His eyes held Lizzie's. He could see the sparkle of tears that made them as blue as the sapphire he knew was inside this tiny box.

'I looked at necklaces,' he continued. 'And bracelets, because I wanted something with diamonds on it.

Diamonds are for ever,' he added. 'And that's how long I will care about you. How long I will love you.'

Lizzie's indrawn breath was audibly shaky. A tear escaped and rolled slowly down the side of her nose. Jack caught it with the pad of his thumb.

'I'm not sure I'm good husband material,' he said. 'My ex-wife would tell you that I'm not. I'm not sure I'm good father material either but there *is* one thing that I'm absolutely sure of.'

'What's that?' Lizzie whispered when he paused to take a slow breath.

'That my life without you would always be hollow. It would be missing a heart.' Jack wanted to smile but the moment was too big. Too important. 'In the end, there was only one gift I could find that could show you how much I love you.'

He opened the box. The ring was a work of art with tiny diamonds surrounding a heart-shaped, blazingly blue sapphire.

Lizzie had her fingers pressed to her lips. Her gaze lifted from the ring nestling in its velvet cushion to meet Jack's eyes.

'Is that…? Are you…?'

'Asking you to marry me? *Oui.*' Jack didn't even notice he was slipping into French to speak words of love. *'Je t'aime, ma chérie. Pour toujours et toujours.'*

Lizzie seemed to understand him perfectly. 'I love you, too,' she whispered. *'So* much. Oh, Jack…of course I'll marry you.'

She threw her arms around his neck and Jack bent his head and kissed her, vowing that he *would* make this work. That he would make her happy. For ever.

He could have kept kissing her for ever but the sound of his phone ringing broke the spell. The unease he felt listening to what Dave Kingsley had to say to him vaporised it completely. A transplant bowel had suddenly become available for Liam.

Why had he done this? Today, of all days?

The anniversary of the day that had marked the end of his marriage to Celine. The Christmas dinner when the call that had taken him back to his hospital had been the final straw.

'I don't have to go,' he told Lizzie. 'Dave can do this surgery himself. He might want my expertise but it isn't essential.'

'But it is,' Lizzie said quietly. 'For Liam. This is the miracle his family has been praying for. You have to go.'

'But it's Christmas Day. Everybody's waiting for us in the dining room. You…and the girls… You are just as important to me as my job, you have to understand that.'

'I do.' Lizzie's smile was misty. 'But I understand what Liam's family are going through as well. It could have been me, Jack. Hoping against hope that a kidney would become available for my precious daughter and that someone—*you*—would be noble enough to postpone your Christmas dinner to make it happen.'

She cradled his face with her hands. 'We'll cope without you for a while. You know why? Because we'll know that you're coming back. That will give us the strength to cope with anything. Any time.'

'You're incredible,' Jack murmured.

She was. She was strong and independent enough

to manage alone if she had to but he knew she would draw on the strength he could give her and *would* give her, at every opportunity he had.

She not only understood his career, she applauded his commitment to it. Loved him for it.

'We'll be here,' Lizzie added softly. 'When you get back. Wherever you are, Jack, we will always be here for you.'

She came to the door with him and he paused long enough for one more kiss.

'I can tell you now,' he said. 'Nelf law definitely does not apply between engaged couples.'

'Oh…' Lizzie caught her bottom lip between her teeth. 'Please…*tell* me what the twins wanted for Christmas.'

Jack bent his head and whispered in her ear.

It was well past the twins' bedtime when Jack returned to the house. They were almost asleep, worn out by the excitement of the day, when Lizzie poked her head around their door.

'Come with me,' she whispered. 'I've found one last present for you.'

Sleepily, holding each other's hands, the girls followed her downstairs in their pyjamas and trailing dressing gowns. Dougal padded in their wake, his new duck toy still in his mouth.

'There.' Lizzie pointed.

Holly looked puzzled. 'Did you put the dolls' house back in its box?'

'Open it,' Lizzie invited. 'And you'll find out.'

Together, the twins pulled the wrapping paper clear of the flaps and they pulled the box open.

Their mouths also fell open.

Jack was sitting inside the huge box.

Lizzie bent down, putting an arm around each of her daughters. 'What was it you asked Father Christmas for, Holly?'

'A daddy,' she whispered.

'That's what Jack's going to be. I'm going to marry him and he will be your daddy. Is that OK?'

'Not just for Christmas?' Misty checked. 'For ever and ever?'

'For ever and ever.' Jack spoke at the same time as Lizzie and they smiled at each other.

Holly climbed into the box with Jack. 'I guess you *are* really a nelf,' she told him kindly. 'Because you can make wishes come true, even if you don't have a green hat.'

Misty squeezed into the box, too.

'Is there room for me?' Lizzie smiled.

'Always.' Jack's smile was all the invitation she would ever need. He held out his hand.

'For ever and *ever*,' the twins shouted.

The noise brought Maggie out from her bedroom. She looked at the members of her family squashed into the box still festooned with strips of Christmas paper.

Her smile was a final gift for the most wonderful Christmas ever.

'Oh, my goodness…it's like *that* now, is it?'

* * * * *

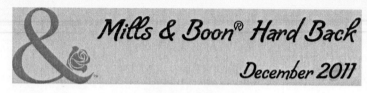

Mills & Boon® *Hard Back*

December 2011

ROMANCE

Jewel in His Crown	Lynne Graham
The Man Every Woman Wants	Miranda Lee
Once a Ferrara Wife...	Sarah Morgan
Not Fit for a King?	Jane Porter
In Bed with a Stranger	India Grey
In a Storm of Scandal	Kim Lawrence
The Call of the Desert	Abby Green
Playing His Dangerous Game	Tina Duncan
How to Win the Dating War	Aimee Carson
Interview with the Daredevil	Nicola Marsh
Snowbound with Her Hero	Rebecca Winters
The Playboy's Gift	Teresa Carpenter
The Tycoon Who Healed Her Heart	Melissa James
Firefighter Under the Mistletoe	Melissa McClone
Flirting with Italian	Liz Fielding
The Inconvenient Laws of Attraction	Trish Wylie
The Night Before Christmas	Alison Roberts
Once a Good Girl...	Wendy S. Marcus

HISTORICAL

The Disappearing Duchess	Anne Herries
Improper Miss Darling	Gail Whitiker
Beauty and the Scarred Hero	Emily May
Butterfly Swords	Jeannie Lin

MEDICAL ROMANCE™

New Doc in Town	Meredith Webber
Orphan Under the Christmas Tree	Meredith Webber
Surgeon in a Wedding Dress	Sue MacKay
The Boy Who Made Them Love Again	Scarlet Wilson

Mills & Boon® Large Print

December 2011

ROMANCE

Bride for Real	Lynne Graham
From Dirt to Diamonds	Julia James
The Thorn in His Side	Kim Lawrence
Fiancée for One Night	Trish Morey
Australia's Maverick Millionaire	Margaret Way
Rescued by the Brooding Tycoon	Lucy Gordon
Swept Off Her Stilettos	Fiona Harper
Mr Right There All Along	Jackie Braun

HISTORICAL

Ravished by the Rake	Louise Allen
The Rake of Hollowhurst Castle	Elizabeth Beacon
Bought for the Harem	Anne Herries
Slave Princess	Juliet Landon

MEDICAL ROMANCE™

Flirting with the Society Doctor	Janice Lynn
When One Night Isn't Enough	Wendy S. Marcus
Melting the Argentine Doctor's Heart	Meredith Webber
Small Town Marriage Miracle	Jennifer Taylor
St Piran's: Prince on the Children's Ward	Sarah Morgan
Harry St Clair: Rogue or Doctor?	Fiona McArthur

Mills & Boon® Hardback

January 2012

ROMANCE

The Man Who Risked It All	Michelle Reid
The Sheikh's Undoing	Sharon Kendrick
The End of her Innocence	Sara Craven
The Talk of Hollywood	Carole Mortimer
Secrets of Castillo del Arco	Trish Morey
Hajar's Hidden Legacy	Maisey Yates
Untouched by His Diamonds	Lucy Ellis
The Secret Sinclair	Cathy Williams
First Time Lucky?	Natalie Anderson
Say It With Diamonds	Lucy King
Master of the Outback	Margaret Way
The Reluctant Princess	Raye Morgan
Daring to Date the Boss	Barbara Wallace
Their Miracle Twins	Nikki Logan
Runaway Bride	Barbara Hannay
We'll Always Have Paris	Jessica Hart
Heart Surgeon, Hero...Husband?	Susan Carlisle
Doctor's Guide to Dating in the Jungle	Tina Beckett

HISTORICAL

The Mysterious Lord Marlowe	Anne Herries
Marrying the Royal Marine	Carla Kelly
A Most Unladylike Adventure	Elizabeth Beacon
Seduced by Her Highland Warrior	Michelle Willingham

MEDICAL

The Boss She Can't Resist	Lucy Clark
Dr Langley: Protector or Playboy?	Joanna Neil
Daredevil and Dr Kate	Leah Martyn
Spring Proposal in Swallowbrook	Abigail Gordon

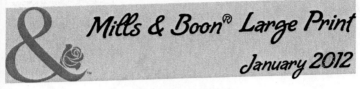

Mills & Boon® Large Print

January 2012

ROMANCE

The Kanellis Scandal	Michelle Reid
Monarch of the Sands	Sharon Kendrick
One Night in the Orient	Robyn Donald
His Poor Little Rich Girl	Melanie Milburne
From Daredevil to Devoted Daddy	Barbara McMahon
Little Cowgirl Needs a Mum	Patricia Thayer
To Wed a Rancher	Myrna Mackenzie
The Secret Princess	Jessica Hart

HISTORICAL

Seduced by the Scoundrel	Louise Allen
Unmasking the Duke's Mistress	Margaret McPhee
To Catch a Husband...	Sarah Mallory
The Highlander's Redemption	Marguerite Kaye

MEDICAL

The Playboy of Harley Street	Anne Fraser
Doctor on the Red Carpet	Anne Fraser
Just One Last Night...	Amy Andrews
Suddenly Single Sophie	Leonie Knight
The Doctor & the Runaway Heiress	Marion Lennox
The Surgeon She Never Forgot	Melanie Milburne

Mills & Boon® Online

Discover more romance at
www.millsandboon.co.uk

- **FREE** online reads
- **Books** up to one month before shops
- **Browse our books** before you buy

...and much more!

For exclusive competitions and instant updates:

 Like us on **facebook.com/romancehq**

 Follow us on **twitter.com/millsandboonuk**

 Join us on **community.millsandboon.co.uk**

Visit us Online

Sign up for our FREE eNewsletter at
www.millsandboon.co.uk

WEB/M&B/RTL4/HB